GLORY

GILLIAN WIGMORE

CALGARY PUBLIC LIBRARY

FEB   2018

Invisible Publishing
Halifax & Picton

Text copyright © Gillian Wigmore, 2017

All rights reserved. No part of this publication may be reproduced or transmitted in any form, by any method, without the prior written consent of the publisher, except by a reviewer, who may use brief excerpts in a review, or, in the case of photocopying in Canada, a licence from Access Copyright.

Library and Archives Canada Cataloguing in Publication

Wigmore, Gillian, 1976-, author
    Glory / Gillian Wigmore.

Issued in print and electronic formats.
ISBN 978-1-926743-98-1 (softcover) | ISBN 978-1-988784-01-4 (EPUB)

    I. Title.

PS8645.I34G56 2017   C813'.6   C2017-905385-X
                                             C2017-905386-8

Edited by Leigh Nash
Cover and interior design by Megan Fildes | Typeset in Laurentian
With thanks to type designer Rod McDonald

Printed and bound in Canada

Invisible Publishing | Halifax & Picton
www.invisiblepublishing.com

We acknowledge the support of the Canada Council for the Arts, which last year invested $20.1 million in writing and publishing throughout Canada.

Canada Council   Conseil des Arts
for the Arts   du Canada

For the Stones of Stone's Bay,
past, present, and future.

And for the Water Girls—Elly,
Fabienne, Laisha, and Jenni.

"Each valley where a cabin has been built has its lore kept alive by the unceasing movement of human lips and tongues. And out of that, like smoke from a smudge—and perhaps no more defined—rises sometimes the figure of a man; not of the real man, perhaps..."
   – HOWARD O'HAGAN, *TAY JOHN*

"He doesn't know
you can't catch
the glory on a hook
and hold on to it.
That when you
fish for the glory
you catch the
darkness too."
   – SHEILA WATSON, *THE DOUBLE HOOK*

CHORUS
Danny Chance, point at Chance Bay

We crossed the Lion's Gate Bridge at daybreak, no traffic, climbing up and out of Vancouver, away from the city, the lower mainland, the only life we'd known so far. We turned a corner and headed north.

We followed the Fraser, kept it on our left flank. It was deep and heavy, flowing back toward the delta and the sea. We left the fields of Chilliwack behind us, and the rough mountains all around spat waterfalls and loomed, impossibly green. We craned our necks looking out the windows. Hope, then the Fraser Canyon, Boston Bar, China Bar, the subterranean seconds when the road was enclosed in concrete tunnels—we hurtled through the sides of mountains.

I sped on the flats, then we watched the traffic flow around us, the Toyota lagging on the long, winding uphills. I thought of our stuff in storage back in the city—how I'd have to hire a U-Haul and do the whole trip again sometime, but I couldn't really imagine a time beyond the interior of the car, the music, Renee humming along when she wasn't crying, the baby jabbering or laughing in the back. I cut the corners on the curves when no one was coming. The Fraser flowed fast and messy below. We stopped at the Devil's Kitchen and watched the rapids.

Renee fell asleep once we left the wet coast behind and the scenery turned dry and the hillside silvered with sage. I snuck glances at her as I drove as fast as I could to make it true that we were leaving. I rolled down the window a crack

1

so I could feel it was real.

We passed Spuzzum, Lytton, Boston Bar, the river pacing us below. Shuttered fruit stands on one side and crumbling cliffs on the other. I marked off time against the power poles, drank water from a bottle nestled between my legs. She woke up outside Cache Creek and we ate takeout hamburgers near the Bonaparte River, me leaning on the car, her sitting sidesaddle in the driver's seat. She nursed Thomas as she ate. I told a stupid joke and she laughed at me. I wanted to catch her smile and keep it.

We barrelled through the Interior Plains. She took photos from the car window of black-crusted rocks, red bluffs, and ignored me. The wind got cold and I shut the window. She piled our coats in her lap and watched the sky: raptors on the updrafts, cumulonimbus piling up in the east. We'd been driving for six hours when we hit 100 Mile House.

"A hundred miles from where?" She had her sunglasses on. I couldn't see if she was joking. The largest cross-country skis in the world, a bird sanctuary, a Tim Horton's, and the highway. We were out the other side and halfway to Williams Lake before we realized it.

I stopped at a pullout near Quesnel for a break. Semi trucks and a camper van with a German flag sticker shared the parking space. I got out to read the Moment in History sign that described the wagon trains and the men who'd defied death on their way to the goldfields. I sat on a cement berm and tried to picture the wagons and donkeys, the men creeping along a dirt road cut into a cliffside, rapids below them, all for the promise of gold.

I looked over at Renee's hair pressed up against the passenger window. The couple in the camper van clambered over their seats into the depths behind them. A trucker lit a smoke and sauntered over.

"Where ya headed?"

"North."

He smoked for a second. "North where? There's a lot of it up there."

"Fort St. James."

He shook his head. "Now why in hell would you go there? Family?"

"Sort of." I shrugged.

He coughed. Spat. Took another drag on his cigarette. "Don't envy you. That place is the goddamn back of beyond." He stooped to peer into the car at Renee sleeping with her mouth open. "That yer wife and kid?"

I nodded. It was a still-new truth. He ground out his cigarette, hiked his pants up, waved at me, and lumbered off.

I watched the clouds swallow the sun before it could set behind the hills. There was nothing on the coast for us. I would make us a home in Fort St. James. My granddad's cabin and the bay on the lake waited for us. I had a job at the mill. I looked at Renee again and felt that zing of hope in my stomach. We were starting something, going north. I felt crazy and hopeful, both.

Renee and the baby slept as I drove. The light disappeared and night came up. I played the Be Good Tanyas quiet on the stereo and watched the eyes of deer in the ditch catch the light of our headlights—quick flares in the dark. When Renee woke up, I pulled over and she took the wheel.

PART ONE

All You Want Is More

RENEE

I felt the ice underneath me melt and seep into my jeans, my coat, even into my hair. I lay on the driveway, my face wet with tears and snot, having just had the first tantrum of my adult life. There was no other word for it.

Thomas cooed in the stroller watching the sky, as I did—the cold, clear April blue—ready for our walk now that I'd freed the stroller wheels. The earth had frozen again over-night, encasing the lower parts of the wheels in solid mud. I'd struggled to free it, sweating through my shirt, swearing and shaking the stroller back and forth until I'd finally lost it and tackled the stroller like a full-sized human opponent. I'd fallen on the handle with all my weight, almost standing Thomas upright in his five-point harness, before the wheels broke loose.

I sat up and wiped my face, pushed my literally dirty blond hair behind my ears, and got up. I was almost glad I had no friends to see me now, or for whom I'd make this funny later in the retelling. I wouldn't tell Danny, that's for sure. There'd been too many moments near-breaking for me—the winter had been so awful, so lonely and unforgiving. I just had to hold it together and spring would come for real—it had to. I didn't know what I'd do if it didn't.

It was late morning by the time I finally followed the driveway through the woods to the road, damp and a little shaky. Tiny frost bridges criss-crossed the puddles. Patches of snow lay in clumps on the road edge and in hollows on the forest floor—dirty white scabs littered with branches and cones. Thomas watched the swallows feint and swoop, and laughed. He seemed to especially love birds, and I tried to care about that—I'd even gone so far as to start building him a mobile for above his crib. I'd cut crow shapes out of felt and weighed them with nickels, but it sat, with my half-finished knitting projects and an abandoned puzzle, on the table we never dined at in our cabin that didn't feel like home.

I squinted in the bright spring sun, marching past the dried thistles and dead grass in the ditch. I saw views through the naked trees I hadn't seen in September, before the snow had fallen and hidden everything—rusted tricycles tangled up with barbed wire in one backyard, a picnic table with an axe head stuck into its charred top in another. I didn't let it mean anything, I just kept going.

I passed the Dream Beaver Pub an hour after I left the cabin. It wasn't open—dark windows watched me balefully, and a large chain wrapped around the door handles was fixed with an oversized lock. I'd never been in. I'd hardly been anywhere. The winter had been a blur of snowstorms rattling our single-pane windows and colic-induced howling—both mine and the baby's.

Now, Thomas seemed to be growing out of his howling, while I was mired. Stoic Danny worked his twelve-hour shifts at the mill and scooped the baby up as soon as he walked in the door. I would go into the bedroom then, lie on his grandparents' bed, and stare at the stacks of books lining the bedroom walls. I hadn't replaced Danny's granddad's Louis L'Amours on the bookshelves, and my books sat in short towers of New Canadian Library and orange Penguin paperbacks on the floor, spines out, waiting for me to be myself again and pick one up for a reread. I hadn't read a book since Thomas was born, eight months and a lifetime ago.

If I managed a walk a day, I was proud. If I only made it as far as the couch, I tried not to fault myself. If it snowed, as it had for October, November, and December through to April, I let myself off the hook. But when the day broke only relatively grey, no snow, no rain, I told myself to get out and walk. Today I was planning to go as far as the grave-yard, then turn around and get home while Thomas was still asleep in the stroller. I had just passed the pub when I heard a car door slam.

"Fucksake." A woman's voice. "Come *on*, Crystal!"

Another door slammed. Two women stood locked in a glare across the hood of an old yellow car. One wore a short white sundress, tight on her hips. Her hair was long, dark, and tangled, and she flipped it over one shoulder, out of her way. The other woman was taller, in jeans and a flannel shirt, a baseball cap over straight black hair. She stood stiff and unmoved by the other woman's shouting. I realized I was staring, and started walking again.

"Hey," the same voice yelled.

I kept going down the road.

"I said hey! You, with the stroller. Come and settle something for us!"

I considered ignoring her, but I hadn't talked to another human outside my family in so long. I couldn't help it—I started toward them, curious about what would come next.

The woman with the curly hair beckoned me closer. "I need your help."

The other woman kept her face turned toward the stand of birch between the pub and the lake. She was slope-shouldered, like she'd been through this before.

I glanced at Thomas, asleep in the stroller. He had that all-out, mid-nap look about him, where thunder could crack and he wouldn't even sigh. I adjusted his blanket, then steered the stroller through the dirt parking lot, toward them.

9

"Good, okay," the woman in the dress said. "I'm Glory. This is my cousin. Going to say hi, Crystal?" She waited, but Crystal said nothing. "Don't worry about her. She's a sour-puss." Crystal didn't flinch. "So, what you're going to do is tell her she's wrong."

"About what?"

Glory hauled the car door open and pushed the seat forward, straining into the back seat to pull out a guitar. It lay uncased on the vinyl.

As soon as Crystal saw the guitar, she started walking down toward the lake.

"Forget about her." Glory cradled the guitar. There was a stippling of nicks under the strings, like cat's paws on the lake when the wind came up. I had no idea what I would hear, but I was eager for it, more excited than I'd been in months. She adjusted the leather strap and thumbed the strings to see if it was in tune. The notes rang out clear from low to high, and the hairs stood up all over my body.

"I wrote this song, but Crystal doesn't think it's any good. You listen and you can tell her how great it is."

The wind stirred the dust in the parking lot, and it stuck to my skin where my sweat had cooled. Crows wheeled above us. Glory played her guitar and sang like no one else I'd ever heard. Her voice was the colour of ashes of roses, smoky and low, gentle and unforgiving at the same time. I felt cold, my breath shallow in my chest. It might have been the wind and the crows, or the birch and their stiff branches revealing the cold lake behind them. It might have been that I'd talked to all of four people in the months since we'd moved to Fort St. James. But whatever it was, I felt like I would never be the same again.

"What do you think?" Glory asked, when she'd finished. She set her guitar against the car and brought both hands up to gather her hair into a bun while she waited for me to answer.

I shook my head. I couldn't talk, for fear of crying. I couldn't say anything, so I looked down toward the birches, where Crystal sat throwing rocks at a log.

"Well?"

The tears brimmed and spilled over.

"That good, hey? That's right. I told you so!" She shouted down at Crystal. Then, to me: "I'm glad you liked it."

I laughed and wiped my eyes with the backs of my hands. My hair, thin and wispy, not long enough to put in a bun, blew around and stuck to my wet face.

She pushed her sunglasses onto the top of her head and smiled. "That's a damn good response to a song. I love making people cry." She shook her head. "It's not too often someone gets a free concert, mind you, but I guess I asked you to listen, didn't I?"

She opened the door and laid her guitar on the back seat. She grabbed a pouch of tobacco from the well of the emergency brake on her way out, then walked around to the back of the car and hopped up to sit on the trunk. She patted the metal beside her.

I collected myself and parked Thomas in the car's shade.

"So, who're you?" she asked, busy rolling the loose tobacco into a slim white torpedo. "Where'd you come from?" She glanced sideways at me, then offered me the new-made cigarette. I took it, and she quickly rolled herself another.

"I'm Renee. I live down the bay." I hopped up on the trunk to sit beside her, and bent to the flame she offered from her lighter. I inhaled and coughed.

She laughed. "Don't smoke?"

I coughed again. "I do, just not much."

"Where round the bay? You mean Chance Bay?"

I cleared my throat and nodded. She whistled.

"Fancy. You must smoke tailor-mades."

We were quiet for a while. I tried to be cool, to still my

shaking hands, to sit there like nothing momentous was happening. She smoked hungrily, then hopped down off the car, tossed her butt into the dirt, and ground it out with her flip-flop. "Crystal!" she shouted.

I got off the trunk, too, and dropped my half-smoked cigarette on the ground. I stood on it so she wouldn't notice I hadn't finished. Everything looked super-etched, like a 1950s postcard of spring in the north: the pub, Crystal coming toward us with the white trunks of the birch trees glowing behind her, her legs unnaturally long in the morning light.

Crystal seemed to consider saying something to her cousin, but turned to me instead. "I don't know what she told you, but I'd be careful if I was you." Her voice was low and her eyes the same dark brown as Glory's. "She don't always tell the truth, and if she does, you can't tell the difference anyway."

"Christ, Crystal, you've hardly ever spoken so much, or so eloquently."

Crystal ignored her. "I'll tell you this, whoever you are: bees look soft to touch but they sting like sons of bitches." She opened the passenger door, got in, and slammed it behind her.

Thomas woke at the sound and cried out.

"Dammit, Crystal, now you done gone and waked the baby!" Glory shouted. To me, she said, "She stole those words from a song I wrote. She doesn't mean it." Glory winked, then turned to get into the car.

"Wait." I didn't want the moment to be over. There was something about Glory, something vivid and alive, and I needed it. "When can I hear you sing again?"

"Tonight. We sing here most Friday nights." She gestured to the pub. "Otherwise I'm over on Southside."

I picked Thomas up out of the stroller. His hair was stuck in sweaty curls. He shivered in the wind and cuddled his head into the crook of my neck. Glory watched us.

"Where are you going, anyway? There's nothing out this way except the graveyard and the train tracks." She eyed me. "You're not running away, are you?"

"No, I'm not running away."

"Now, that is a bald lie, missy. Every single one of us is running away, just at different speeds. Me, for instance, I'll be gone by this time next year. Gone, gone, gone."

She was interrupted by the car horn. Crystal sat back in her seat and glared out the windshield. Thomas howled in my ear.

"That girl is so touchy!" Glory grinned. Her short dress flapped around her thighs and she pulled her sunglasses on. "If you want to hear us play, you'd better do it soon." She climbed into the car.

She backed the yellow car up so the tires spun and spit gravel. I hugged Thomas close and turned my back to the grit in the air. Glory screeched to a stop just before the road and shouted back, "The highway's that way!" and honked her horn. I could see her bare arm waving as she drove off.

When the dust settled, and I had Thomas strapped back into the stroller with his soother in his mouth and his blanket in his fist, I felt hollow. I stood and watched the lake slap and jostle the shore, rougher than it had been when I'd left it behind in Chance Bay that morning. It almost wasn't morning anymore. I started walking.

I wasn't running away, but that's what got us here—we'd run from the coast, from houses we'd never afford, jobs we couldn't compete for despite degrees and experience. We'd come north to have a chance at a new life, one almost ready-made in Danny's dad's hometown, in the cabin his grandfather built on a bay named for his family, in a fully furnished cabin Danny inherited. It wasn't what I'd expected, though—not the town, the cabin. Not that I'd known what to expect. Remembering leaving Vancouver felt like digging a knuckle into a bruise—the city receding behind us as we drove across the bridge into North Van, then through the coast mountains toward the wilds of the Interior. I could still feel the ache of leaving, but part of it was the memory of my breasts near to explosion with mastitis.

It was fall. I remembered the trees all orange and brown, a highway pullout with a pond. I saw mallards, a dilapidated dock, but I didn't really see them. I had my teeth clenched. I sat in the car and swore.

"You have to let him suck," Danny said.

"It hurts too much."

I'd held my breasts from underneath and they were like two heads, so heavy, so hard. I wished for breast skulls. I wished I'd never have to feed anything from them again. I wished I was a flat-chested kid in a field, lying on her back staring at the sky. I'd been that kid once. Now my chest was a grotesquery that stung like an open wound.

Danny had walked the baby away from the car a few steps, then walked back. I leaned my head against the headrest on the passenger side watching his skinny hips, the light glinting off his glasses every time he turned. I had mastitis. I'd looked it up. It affected cows, goats, anything with udders.

"Why is it happening?" Danny tried to get the baby to want the soother, jiggling it around his wet lips like he hadn't already been rejecting it for half an hour. Thomas wailed around it, punching his baby fists in the air.

"I didn't feed him enough. We were driving. No, we were moving and then we were driving. Yesterday and the day before and the day before we were distracted from the schedule." The schedule had been my lifeline. Then moving was. I let the baby sleep so I could pack more. I let him finish nursing even if I knew he wasn't really done. Sometimes I hadn't offered him both breasts. I glanced at my bare chest and away. Mountains of pain. Eruptions of scalding, black awful. I didn't care who saw them in this parking lot half-way to nowhere.

"Can we try again? He's so hungry."

I closed my eyes. "Yes. But then we're stopping in the next town for formula. And painkillers. And vodka."

"You're a good mother, you know."

I'd kept my eyes closed. He was kind but not perceptive. I held out my arms for the baby.

"Do you need something to bite down on?"

That made me open my eyes. He was also funny, Danny. Sometimes he was very funny, I remembered, back when we weren't parents. I eyed him. "Just get me an apple from the bag. And my notebook. Please." I didn't want to write anything, I just wanted it near—fat with ephemera, book-marks and ticket stubs, poems and photos and thoughts. It was my security blanket.

Thomas rooted around my nipple, wild for the smell of milk coming off me. I held my breath and angled his mouth, and the pain when he latched sent a black spike through my head. I felt it through my bowels and sat stiff. I had to con-sciously try and let the milk flow, to soften my arms for him, to be a dispenser of nourishment, not a woman with flames in her chest, not a woman whose breasts had been replaced with boulders ready to burst from her skin.

Danny came back with an apple and my brick of a note-book and set them on my lap. He picked up my shirt from the ground where I'd thrown it, shook it out, and wiped the tears off my face. He crouched next to me, stroking my hair. He stayed close, pressed his finger into my shoulder for a long second. You, it meant. He'd always done it, ever since the beginning, though I couldn't remember when he start-ed and I couldn't say why I knew what it meant. Had he explained it to me? I didn't know. I breathed and Thomas sucked and the highway hummed with traffic. I looked past Danny and fixed my eyes on a tilted outhouse. Birds swooped low over the pond next to it, feasting on mosquitoes, and slowly I relaxed my shoulder blades, loosened my jaw, stroked the soft skin on the baby's forehead. I loved his forehead. It was my favourite place to kiss.

Evening fell while he nursed. I could feel my breasts softening, and when he was finished they were almost back to normal. The ducts deep inside them still ached, and I could feel swelling, still, right back into my armpits, but I managed to put on a shirt while Danny strapped Thomas into his car seat. My bra stayed on the floor mat and I kept my eyes from it. I worked my phone for a minute.

"Cabbage leaves. That's what we need," I told Danny when he got in the car.

"Cabbage leaves? Maybe monkey's paws, too?"

I snorted. "How much further?"

"Ten k to the next town. Two more hours to Fort St. James."

"Two hours to the middle of nowhere."

"You might like it better if you didn't call it that. It's nice. All my best childhood memories are there."

I bit into my apple. "It's an Adventure, right?"

"Yep. Affordable and New."

"A Fresh Start." These were the words we used to explain it—to ourselves, to our friends in the city who couldn't understand our leaving. It was a mantra and something to pin my mind to.

"We already own our own home there. Can't say that in Vancouver. No one can say that in Vancouver."

"But is it really a home?" I broke the chain of self-comfort. "It's a cabin." I rolled down my window and threw the apple core out toward the dark fields.

"It's something. And it's ours. Just like this car. Just like this family." That was Danny's role: Reminder of Things So My Questions Don't Wreck the Fairy Tale.

I watched out the window even though the world was becoming indistinct in the dusk. I could feel the fever thrumming in my body, the fields and forests passing too fast. I closed my eyes and let sleep court me. Danny talked on about our destination, the quality of the road, about other drivers, animals in the ditch, and I let it rumble over me, just like the highway rumbled under me. Part of me was still in my bed in our old apartment in Vancouver. I imagined myself a ghost there. Some other couple in some other bed would lie down on my ghostly form and not know it. It felt like my breasts were glowing red.

I interrupted him by lifting a hand. "Can you see the heat coming off me? Like asphalt in the summer?"

"No," he laughed.

"Turn up the music. I need distraction."

"I'm not distraction enough?"

"Not from the calibre of my misery." I thought about that for a second. I softened it for him. "But close."

In Prince George, we rented a room. Danny wasn't sure about driving on in the night with me in my condition (mastitis, misery). I told him he just didn't know the way to his grandpa's cabin. He pretended I wasn't talking. Thomas slept all the way into town, up the stairs in his car seat, and into the motel room, which smelled like cigarette smoke and boiled sheets. It made me nervous, the baby sleeping, because it meant he would wake up at some point and the cycle would begin again. I needed the Advil to have kicked in so I could stand the nursing. Danny said four extra-strength pills were too many, that they would go in the milk and Thomas would drink it, but I told him he wasn't inside my body and he didn't have to have a kid sucking on him like the world's biggest tick. He said that wasn't funny. I closed my eyes again, which was stupid because I was standing in the middle of a dinky motel room at the Gateway to the North, which then made me cry because I'd never felt so far from home, even when I was travelling in Europe or South America, even in my dreams.

In the morning, Danny brought coffee and doughnuts to me while I nursed and swore. Thomas rolled off my nipple at the sound of his dad's voice and broke out beaming, milk streaming out of his toothless mouth.

"Thank god he's got no teeth."

"Does it feel any better? They look sort of smaller and less solid." He meant my breasts. He reached to stroke one, so I intercepted his hand and held it, squeezing it to let him think that was better than touching me. Thomas clambered back on my boob, his spiked, starfish hands all over my bare chest. I remembered my dad's purebred lab sheepishly trying to escape the enclosure she shared with her puppies, her scratched and bleeding dugs slapping the barrier as she stepped over it. I sent my love back to her too late; I would never have locked her in there with them had I known.

I ate my doughnut: a long john, my favourite, then I looked in the bag hopefully, and saw Danny had bought me another. He smiled through his bite, happy to have pleased me.

Prince George turned out to be bigger than I'd thought. It was Saturday, I remember. We put Thomas in the baby carrier—a wrap that I still hadn't mastered on my own. Danny wound it around me while I clutched the squirming baby to my front. I liked having my hands free and feeling like the baby was contained, but there was an unsettling element in his being tied to me. If I could figure out how it worked, I could strap him to Danny, and they would both like that, I knew.

We put on our sunglasses and put a hat on the baby and

went out into the wind and grit of downtown Prince George in September. This would become my defining opinion of the city—dirt and gorgeousness in equal measure: fresh produce and cheerful stall-minders, blue sky above low buildings, boarded-up storefronts, white and Indigenous people in dust-coloured, many-layered clothing, congregating on benches and in alleys, trees in full fall leaf. I imagined us from above or behind, as if seen through a lens and we were typical and beautiful in our dailiness. Danny bought jerky and honey with cash. I ate a fresh bun. The painkillers worked and my breasts subsided, and when we got in the car to drive the rest of the way I was calm, becalmed, submissive to the current. I watched the scenery pass like an unnarrated nature film. Thomas slept in the back, Danny drove, and I waved goodbye to Mr. P.G. like he wasn't a silly, giant wooden man at the edge of the last city in northern BC, but like a dad or a kind uncle who'd bought a lollipop to calm me.

In Vanderhoof there was a restaurant with lemon meringue pie where women wore white netted caps on the backs of their heads and dresses that brushed the floor. The meringue was delicious. I nursed Thomas in the shade of a tree, counting out loud the whole time to take my mind off the bolts of pain that broke through the barrier of the meds.

I read the descriptions of provincial parks to Danny while he drove.

"Liard. Where is that even?"

I checked. "Four hundred and eleven kilometres from Dease Lake."

"How can that still be in the province? That would mean it takes three days to drive from Vancouver to the Yukon."

"It does. And it takes two days to drive from Vancouver to the cabin."

"You could do it in one."

"Do you think anyone will visit us?"

"They said they would. Tanya said so. And Alison."

I'd stared out the window at a creek creeping through a marshy field. Tanya wouldn't come. There would be nowhere to shop. Alison said all kinds of things she didn't mean. I remembered the shower they threw for me before Thomas was born, all the women in Tanya's apartment. All of them drinking wine except me. The gifts ridiculous or inappropriate. How I'd realized in the middle of the party that the idea of a baby would stay abstract for them. Suddenly they'd seemed outlined in black—their short skirts, everyone's hair up off their necks in the heat of the evening, Tanya slapping our friend Elise on the thigh and bending at the waist while she laughed. They'd all complimented me on how thin I'd stayed through the pregnancy. They bought me cute T-shirts and gourmet tea. They'd asked how Danny was handling it.

My phone hadn't buzzed since the goodbye texts. Now I was abstract, too. How could these single women in their early twenties, my own age, with jobs and dates and downtown lives, imagine my new life when I could hardly fathom it, and I was living it? I felt nauseous and rolled my window down.

"You okay, Ren?"

I didn't answer.

"I could stop."

I waved him away.

"We're almost there."

Where was there? Cows stood hock-deep in creek water, crows lined the crossbars on power poles. We turned right at an intersection between two fields—the highway we left carrying on over the hundreds of kilometres to the Pacific, the highway we followed stretching out in front of us. I saw on the map that it ended in Fort St. James.

"There are fish in that lake as big as sharks, Renee. They live for a hundred years. They're like dinosaurs."

"I hate sharks."

"Sturgeon are bottom-feeders. They eat stuff like weeds and garbage off the bottom. The thing is, native people there have fished them for generations. And there'd be a huge celebration when they caught one."

"That would be like eating a grandfather. A hundred-year-old fish. Yuck. And I don't think you say native people, I think you're supposed to say Indigenous. Or maybe First Nations? I don't know."

Danny shrugged. "My grandpa always said Carrier. The Carrier people live up here. My dad said Indian, but what did he know? Anyway, Pope Mountain is the one on the north side, where we'll be. There's a trail to the top. I climbed it with my grandpa when I was five. He was so proud of me. I remember the view. Or maybe I'm remembering another view."

We'd sold our bikes, our packs, the toaster, and the microwave. I kept the popcorn maker. We'd never bought a crib because we knew we'd be leaving, so Thomas slept with us or in a pack-away playpen. We felt so sensible, on schedule, like we had it figured out and everyone else was stupid for not understanding. Didn't they realize that $2,000 rent on a one-bedroom apartment was ridiculous? We had five acres waiting for us in the north. We could fish in the lake at the bottom of our deck stairs. We could maybe have a garden.

Danny created a story of us that he recited in the months and weeks leading up to our leaving. But the moments he wasn't talking, when I was on my own in the supermarket or out on a quick trip for more moving boxes, doubts crept in. Could we buy espresso up there? Or, when I was thinking like a grown-up: would there be a

21

hospital? Would we have a doctor?

The map of northern BC is a blue-veined expanse freckled with lakes and more lakes. Names that made me laugh or that were too tough to sound out were dots along the highway, spaced far apart, impossible to imagine. I asked Danny to pronounce them and then, when we drove through Lytton, Clinton, Cache Creek, and Quesnel, I stared around me for clues in their strange ordinariness: gas stations and kids on the street corners smoking cigarettes. No indication in the benches and civic signs that I was on a journey into the wild—these were just normal Canadian towns. There were coffee shops that sold espresso. There were movie theatres showing movies not too out of date. The sky looked superblue beyond the Quonset huts and cinder-block warehouses, the rivers picturesque beside cookie-cutter houses and cute little rural schools. I'd looked back to check the baby when we were five hours out of Vancouver and caught sight of a train bridge behind us in the distance like a pencil drawing of the American West. It was momentous and simple at the same time. Dizziness overcame me every time I turned my head. I complained so much Danny did all the driving. And then the mastitis.

"I remember this." Danny scanned the land ahead of us, his voice quiet, almost reverent. "I remember this bridge. This is the Nechako River. People swim here. I swam here once with Dad and Jimmy." I preferred not to look at the river because of his druggie brother Jimmy, but I could feel it was old, and real, and bigger than anything in my head—it would outlast me and my opinion of Jimmy.

We crossed the bridge, drove up the other side of the valley and onto a plateau. The sky stretched limitless in all directions. East between the edges of two huge fields, then north again, we drove and I watched a raptor rising on a thermal, round and round, up and up.

"This is Braeside. I remember my grandpa saying so. Farming country. There used to be a huge barn there, where those trees are. Look at that tractor. Jesus, that's huge. This is Twelve Mile Hill. See the sign?"

I saw the sign. I saw a power station and a coyote in the ditch. Danny kept talking. Names and farms fell away behind us. We drove north, all uphill, it felt, closer and closer to the clouds. My eyes were heavy behind my sunglasses, the car hot in the afternoon sun, the comfort of Danny's voice over the drone of the engine. I woke suddenly, thrown against my seat belt, the weight of the car's momentum crushing me into the webbing. I heard the tires screech, Danny's shout and Thomas's holler. Three bears scampered off the highway into the brush at the side of the road.

"They came out of nowhere!"

I had my seat belt off, clambering over the seat to get to the baby. I jostled my breast on the headrest, wincing at the pain, and got Thomas's soother back in his mouth. He settled immediately. He closed his eyes. I sat back. Danny held his hands up and we watched them tremble.

"You said there'd be wildlife," I tried to joke.

"I think I need a minute. Can you drive?" He pulled onto the shoulder, stopped the engine, and got out. He walked away from us up the highway. No cars came. No cars, and no cars. I looked back behind us and saw nothing. I got out.

It smelled like hot, dry grass. It was so still, I heard the rustle of the needles on the roadside trees. I called his name. He turned and waved at me but didn't come back.

I left the passenger door open and picked my way down into the ditch. A thin runnel of water wet the plants at the bottom. I hopped over it and made my way up the bank toward the small green baby pine at the top. I recognized the long needles from Girl Guide sleep-away camp. I squatted behind a spindly tree, pulling my pants down so I could crouch and pee in the hot sun. Then a car came. Four faces watched me as it drove past. They pointed and waved but no sound reached me from behind the window glass. The sun warmed my bare back. I blushed all over.

That's how it came to be me driving into Fort St. James, dizzy, slightly feverish, embarrassed, on a hot September day, leaking from the nipples because we'd missed a feed, Danny still hysterical with laughter at my having been caught with my pants down, Thomas fussing in the back. "Dog Creek," Danny said. We slowed to ninety, minding the speed limit posted on the signs, then slowed to seventy. Stuart River, he said, and I saw it: the lake, stretching all the way to the horizon. We drove onto the bridge and I felt its yawning pull, a great emptiness: lake on one side, river on the other, me trying to keep between the lines while my eyes darted all over, trying to take it all in. A lake like the ocean.

"You didn't tell me," I said.

"I tried. There aren't words for it."

I tried, too. There weren't. Thomas wailed in the back for milk. "Can you lead us home from here?"

"I think so," he'd said. "Just follow the shore."

A hard winter later, I walked the empty road we'd first driven that fall, heavy with memories of leaving and arriving. I was sweating in my clothes again, the sun having broken through the clouds. I could feel the prickle of milk in my breasts—it was almost time for Thomas to wake. I picked up my pace, my steps purposeful and swift, but I had something new to remember now—maybe a new friend. Glory. I tasted her name in my mouth. It felt like a new beginning.

CHORUS
Dan Bebenall, Dream Beaver Pub

Oh, sure I know Glory. She's been working at the pub for years. She makes your eyes feel better after you've been staring at what's her name, the bartender, Sandy.

Glory's alright. I like it when she plays on Friday nights. I'm usually here, anyway, but I'd come up just for that. She's a bit of a kook, with those short skirts and boots, but if you've had a few, she's real pretty. Like not-from-here pretty. She wears lots of eye makeup and she's got this real dark hair and skin. Lots of girls up here have dark skin, but Glory, she's cut from different cloth.

Oh, I don't mean she's crazy or nothing. She's just not like some of them other bar girls. And she's a bar girl, alright. You don't see her at the grocery store or the drugstore. Maybe the cold beer and wine, but other than that, you see her here at the pub, at the Cabaret, or maybe at a party. And she can be wild! I seen her dancing on a table at Tom Reid's in a skirt with no panties on—three sheets to the wind! And cranky! Man. That girl could strip the skin off anyone— bangs her fist on the table until whoever she's firing off at slinks away. Glory don't suffer fools gladly. She'll tell you you're an ass, then thank you to buy her next drink.

No, I don't usually have much tolerance for snarky women. Glory can sing, though. I'm a country man myself. Not that new rock 'n' roll country. I like a Hank Williams song, or Patsy Cline. My dad listened to that stuff back in the olden days and it means something to me. I heard Glory sing some old sad country song just a while ago and I cried. Serious. I sat here at the bar, and I wasn't the only one, neither.

Glory sings all that folk stuff and she sings too damn much Bob Dylan, but she can sing a sweet country song like it was her who wrote it, like her own heart was breaking and nothing could stop it. I'll tell you something. You look around the bar during one of those songs and no other woman exists. She could have her pick of men. Yeah, I heard those rumours, too. No telling who her little girl's daddy is. The word around town isn't pretty.

Sounds like I've done a study, hey? I've spent a lot of time on this stool, a lot of time watching people walk by, slap each other on the back, buy each other drinks. I'm here through every season, seen every type who saunters in—the dirty tree planters flush with cash and ordering water, the loggers just in from the bush leaving stupid big tips for the girls and pinching their asses if they get too near, old guys like me. I never said I was much of a catch, but I know this place and, yes, I know Glory some. Enough to put a fiver in her guitar case every few months, but I know enough to leave her alone, too.

RENEE

The radio voices prattled while I ate canned soup, nursed the baby, and put him down for his nap. The CBC played non-stop from the tinny little radio I'd found in the shed. I thought maybe it would improve my lonely mind, but I retained nothing of the documentaries and new stories. I'd tried to read or sleep while Thomas slept, but my mind would never settle. I'd tried to write letters, but failed. What would I say? We had no W-Fi, so email was out of the question. There was a computer with Internet access at Chow's Diner, but it was busy all the time, plus it was in town. The only answer for blank midday hours were yoga videos, and smug Rodney Yee rubbed me the wrong way, so I left the radio on to fill the room with living voices and went out to the deck. The steps were only a memory under a lumpy, treacherous coating of ice and snow. It had snowed, melted, frozen, and snowed again so many times that spring felt like a hurtful lie. How could the roads be clear and the ice almost off the lake while our stairs were still covered with snow? It didn't make sense.

I got the chipper from where it leaned against the side of the cabin. I slammed the blade into the top step and an ice chunk the size of a pumpkin broke off and fell down the slope toward the lake. Satisfaction surged in me. I chipped the melted snow off the top deck and worked my way down the stairs. I chopped and smashed and kicked the chunks of ice, and it was pleasing to see the wet wood emerge after a month of pussyfooting around.

I heard something and stopped. The ice on the lake shifted and moaned. It was thinner than yesterday. The Ski-Doo tracks were darker, going from grey shadows on the snow to precise black lines stretching off toward the blue horizon. The horizon was different, too, I thought, less a white line in the distance and more a deep blue wall. The lake amazed me. I'd seen the ocean-sized expanse of it ice up overnight, and still couldn't believe it. I'd stood mid-lake at night listening to it groan while stars whirled in the black sky above. I'd watched a truck drive across a week ago and I'd stopped breathing. The ice held. It was April and the thermometer in my body was set to southern time—the world should be green and blooming. My cells ached for it.

I scanned the ice for change and thought about Danny. I tried to listen to him talk about his job—he'd say it was loud at the mill; so-and-so was a blowhard; this one guy had so much seniority he did nothing but watch movies all day; he liked one guy a lot—Bud, was it? Bob. No, Bud. I listened, but I couldn't really imagine the people or the place. Danny said he liked it, working at the mill, and I wondered about that but didn't ask how he could pack his sharp and critical brain up in his hard hat and settle down to this existence.

I listened, but I was fighting panic, as usual, trying to appear calm while a lightning storm raged inside me. It was impossible to reconcile where we were with where we'd been, or where I'd thought we'd have gone. I was going to be a writer. I was going to travel, to see great things, and share them with the world. He was going to be a professor, I'd thought. Instead, he worked at a mill, and I wallowed, fearful and hateful and small.

In my first year of university, I'd wanted to teach philosophy. I read ahead in the texts and challenged the professor on every point. It was introductory philosophy, not difficult, but I loved the way my brain felt bigger each time I learned a new term and applied it cavalierly in class before we'd been taught the definition. Danny had sat the next row over. I knew he had his eye on me. I let him work the courage up to talk to me, and when he did, just before he opened his mouth, I put my hand on his and said, "Let's get coffee." We were friends before we were lovers—good friends. For three years, while I changed my mind about majors and minors before finally settling into my English degree, he listened to me, paid for my movies, walked me to class. We had witty repartee; he made me laugh, I made him roll his eyes. We were lovers, eventually, because he was so precious and earnest, and I couldn't resist the eye-rolling. We got pregnant because I was careless.

"What do you want to do?" he'd asked. It was Christmas break, our last year of undergrad.

All the scenarios rushed through my head: I was pro-choice; I wanted a baby; I would get an abortion; I could be a mother.

"We'll do whatever you want," he'd said.

I couldn't believe him. What about his degree? My degree? What would we live on?

"Let's do this together," he'd said. We were on the phone. I was at my dad's condo in Coal Harbour, in the dark of the living room. He was in his apartment across town. I could hear him breathing. I could picture his face. I remembered lying on his mattress when we'd first started sleeping together, how he'd told me about his father, drunk in the morning and throwing eggs at him from the porch, how he was laughing when he'd started the story and crying by the end of it. He had his head on my chest, my heartbeat audible to both of us. I remembered the smell of his clean hair. I wanted always to hold him, to be the only one who saw him cry.

"Okay," I said, and suddenly we were parents-to-be. Separate, immediately, from all our friends and fellow students, though we did graduate, but we were already living in an afterward none of them could imagine.

We lived in his little apartment with the weevils and roll-up bugs. His dad died in July. Thomas was born in August. He had the idea to head north sometime in between.

From where I sat, I could see black patches on the lake far out from shore and I wondered if these were open water. I climbed the clean stairs and set the ice pick aside, retrieved cigarettes and a lighter from a plastic baggy in the woodpile, and climbed up to sit on the picnic table to watch what the weather would do next. I thought it might storm.

There was something in the light that made me uneasy. I looked far down the lake to where it narrowed, and the mountains on the north side curved almost all the way around to touch the low hills on the south side. Between the shoulders of land, the sky was navy blue going on black. The wind, if anything, was getting warmer, and although I thought about putting my sweater back on, it was mesmerizing to finally sit outside without a toque and mittens and scarf. The dark sky moved east, toward me— the lake was like a funnel that drew the weather right to the cabin, perched where it was in the crook of the bay. I'd stood on the point when we'd arrived in the fall, shaken and amazed, the wind howling and rain pelting out of a pitch-black sky.

I smoked the cigarette down to the filter and put the butt down a crack in the deck. I stowed the packet and lighter. I still had enough of a sweat going that I didn't need my sweater, so I left it and took up the ice chipper again to get the parts I'd missed. I slammed the flat of the blade into a hunk of ice and pried it loose, sending shards skittering in all directions. I smashed the chipper down again and again. Soon, my breath was coming in gasps, and the gasps made me think of sex. I was suddenly furious that sex was on my mind, that Danny had stopped reaching for me in bed, even though it was my fault. I never had cause to roll away, but I did it, anyway. Every time.

When I used to lie awake, naked and waiting for the touch of his hand, I'd thought it would always be like that: anticipation and consummation. There were nights of climbing his body like it was a dock ladder. There'd been mornings of trying to leave the bed and failing.

I rode him like he was a fine specimen of horseflesh sixteen hands high. I said, "Keep it steady," "Hold still." I called him "boy." I lay down with him, intending never to get up.

There were nights of words and glasses of water and sleep, but I always knew I could have him just by fitting my butt into his lap when we lay side by side. I could be on the bus and think of his fingers and be wet instantly, wanting to be back at the apartment, pulling down his shorts. I had the idea that this wanting and having was permanent.

Now each night I lay beside him, crystallized: every particle of me columnar and hard and cold. Somewhere in the winter, I'd lost him. If I thought of his fingers, it was how they gripped the steering wheel while he drove us to town. It was when they wiped the baby's face with a cloth. I thought of sex and couldn't remember ever wanting to be so penetrable.

He'd looked at me at breakfast this morning, and I knew he was confused. Why had it turned off? Could I turn it back on again? I didn't know. My skin felt brittle over the angles of my bones, and I couldn't bear him to touch me. Even in that regard, I was a failure: a mother who couldn't love her son enough, a wife who wouldn't open up to her husband, even for sex. I was broken and it made me want to cry. I shook my head. I wouldn't start that again. I felt like I'd been crying for days.

I stomped my feet and turned to go in the cabin. I grabbed the wooden handle on the sliding door and pulled, but it stuck. It wouldn't open. I tried again. I tugged on it and it creaked against my weight, but didn't give. I looked through the window at the baby monitor on the counter where I'd left it. The light flashed—a steady blinking eye in the gloom—but I felt panic welling. I grabbed the handle and pulled hard. I grunted, heaving and tugging, doing nothing to the door, the baby monitor flashing away. I yelled and stopped and stepped back.

I wound up and kicked the door hard on its frame, then kicked it again and again, my winter boot bouncing off the wood, a spike of sharp pain driving through my foot with each blow. I was sobbing. I kicked until I thought my toes would break. I grabbed the handle again and rattled. I heard a soft thunk. I gulped air. I tried the door again and it slid open.

I stood, panting at the threshold. Thomas's amplified breaths came steady and slow, but the fury I'd built up had made me light-headed. My cheeks burned. I stared around the empty room, at the dusty clock showing half past three and the couch where my housecoat still lay in a heap on the seat, a dirty coffee cup on the floor. I didn't move. The radio droned on. I couldn't get in and then I could. I thought about that. The panic was real, my need to get to Thomas was like something I'd read in a book: a mama-bear response. That was the right response, I thought, and I was glad I'd had it, but I was empty now, and that wasn't right. All the feeling in me had puddled and slid away down the cleared stairs. I stood on the doorstep until my heart beat normally again, then I stepped carefully inside.

CHORUS
Lana Delmont, Pentecostal Church foyer

I heard that, too. Some people moved into Roy's old cabin on Chance Bay. Me and Jim went past there last fall before the ice come on, and there was a fire in the stove, smoking like a you-know-what. We were headed out to close up our place on Jenny Cho Island and we seen the smoke and come in close to shore in the boat to see. Lulu at the Petro-Can said some family was living there but she didn't know any more than that. At choir the other night, I heard they was American. Also heard that they was on the run from something, like some bad tragedy, but Jim said they were probably bank robbers or those pot farmers growing marijuana up in the bushes under the mountain.

It looked just same as ever, with the porch tilting down to the lake. They got an old wood table and some chairs on the deck and the woodpile's been built up some. Not so wet and musty-looking, maybe, 'cause they got a car in the clearing, but mostly the same as when Roy lived there himself.

That was always a lonely place. No one out there but Roy and his dog. No one coming to visit or stay, and him with the best view on the north side. Sad place. Roy's wife dead, his boys gone. Roy living out there till, what? He died? Just gone one day. I should ask Lulu about that. She might know that story about old Roy.

So, anyways, me and Jim was boating and we saw that tippy-roof cabin with smoke coming out of the chimney and I says to Jim, "Who'd live there?" and he says, "Ghosts." Just like that. Gave me a chill. "Ghosts." Could almost believe it.

RENEE

You couldn't call the deer path a trail, really. I pushed through the willow shoots, my sweater sticking on branches, burrs latching onto my pants and socks. I followed the faint path through the bushes between our house and the neighbours' with Thomas in my arms, just wrapped in a blanket because I was in too much of a rush to put his snowsuit on. He cooed and laughed. Everything was an adventure for him. I held the branches back from whipping him in the face and tried to quell my panic.

People said *nestled* when they talked about a cabin: nestled in among the trees. They said *quaint, rustic, hand*-hewn. About this one I would say *haunted. Frightened* would work, too. The trees were so big they made the cabin look like it was cowering, like it had crawled to the cliff edge to get away from the hundred-year-old firs that stood around it and all the way up Pope Mountain—huge Douglas fir, brambles of dogwood and Labrador tea, spruce that raced each other for the sky—everything was overgrown. It made me feel miniature and stupid—like I'd only been living long enough to know my own unhappiness, nothing else, nothing like these tree sentinels who'd seen centuries. I knew they were old because I'd seen a photo of Danny's granddad standing next to a baby spruce in front of a shack, and that shack was our cabin, and that spruce was now taller than a telephone pole.

There were so few clues about his grandparents. I had

plenty of time to look—there were no boxes of love letters or journals or diaries anywhere in the cabin that described the feeling of the place. It was an awful feeling and I felt it all the time: the cold seeping out of the bathroom despite the morning sun that made its way through the trees to the window; the blue, blue of the bedroom; the lethargy in my bones when I dragged myself out of bed to see to the baby, the tears that overcame me when I crept back. There were only four rooms in the cabin and I hated each one.

The kitchen could be okay at certain times of day. Mid-morning and mid-afternoon there were almost nice—Thomas playing on the rug in front of the windows, the lake beyond, the radio prattling while I cooked or made tea or tried to fit pieces of grass or flower or cow together in the endless puzzle on the dining table. I could sit on the couch while the kettle boiled and read a book and still be within steps of the stove. A kettle boiling was a homey sound. But come four o'clock, it changed—the whistle of the kettle was an assault that pierced my brain. Four o'clock was the black time. If the baby was still sleeping, I got him up for company. But I scared myself. I couldn't be sure I wouldn't slap Thomas's hand if he reached for my cup and spilled tea on my shirt. I couldn't be sure that just because I dropped a cup, or lost a game of solitaire, or burned the food to the bottom of the pan, I wouldn't walk out the front door and never come back. Was I broken? Or just exhausted? I didn't know, but I couldn't tell Danny about it. All the words I tried came out wrong, like complaints or self-pity. Instead, I held Thomas close, turned the radio loud, made more and more elaborate dinners from the simple things I could get at Overwaitea Foods. Four o'clock was my nemesis. This wasn't the first time I'd found myself plowing through the bush to the Swannells' house.

Thank goodness they were retired. They were always glad to give us cookies and see Thomas blow spit bubbles and jabber. I melted into a stiff chair in their sitting room and fiddled with my cup and saucer, watching the same view as ours, only one lot over. While they laughed and played with the baby, I drank my tea and listened to the fire crackle. I took in the little gold-framed oil paintings and stiff black-and-white photos of Swannell ancestors, and I smiled and answered their questions, but I kept one eye on the lake and an ear out for the sound of the car.

Mrs. Swannell—Rosie, she said to call her—watched me closely. She let Thomas tug on the string of beads that held her glasses around her neck. Jim Swannell filled the living room with weather commentary, but I felt like Mrs. Swannell could see me trying to hold it together. If I didn't have to escape the cabin I wouldn't have gone to them—I was terrified she'd say the thing that would undo my careful front and I'd come tumbling down. It had taken all my evasive skills to avoid spending Christmas dinner with them.

Christmas came and we weathered it alone. We had nothing prepared—no decorations, no traditions, not even a plan. I would have preferred not to celebrate, but Danny was a do-it-for-the-sake-of-doing-it kind of guy; our uncarved Halloween pumpkins were still out there under the snow, flat and rotten piles of almost and didn't.

Danny built a bonfire on Christmas Eve. He started with the blowdown from the fir trees ringing the cabin, rounds from the old woodpile, and branches on the shore that washed up last year, and it ended up an eight-foot monster pile of wood on the beach. I watched him build it from the kitchen window. His breath followed him like a thought bubble as he hauled wood and threw it higher and higher up the pile. I could see him getting hotter; his hair, plastered to his head, turning straggly and dark. It was getting so long it brushed the collar of his woolen shirt and mingled with his beard.

Thomas had napped all that afternoon. When Danny came in, it was dark, the black time in full swing, and I had swapped out my tea for whisky. I'd cleaned the cabin while he worked. I'd been a good wife. I swept out the dark corners and wiped down the counters. The tea towels hung straight and soup was on the stove. He was careful not to make too big a deal about it, but I could tell he was pleased—he raised his eyebrows and nodded, his lips bent in a smile. He wanted me to be okay. I wished I could tell him I was. Instead, I opened a beer for him while he unwound his scarf and took off his boots. I handed it to him and I wanted to do more.

"Can I cut your hair for you?"

He fingered the damp strands at his neck as he drank. "It's long, isn't it? Have you cut hair before?"

"No, but I can figure it out."

I pulled the kitchen rug away and sat him on a stool on the empty floor. He took off his shirt and I grabbed a comb and all the scissors we had: nail scissors, kitchen scissors, paper scissors, pinking shears—those were a joke. He smiled when he saw them.

His skin was the colour of stained wood in the firebox's glow. The overhead light was low. I placed a fingertip on his crown and he complied, bending his neck, bowing chin to chest. I took a last sip of whisky and set the cup down, then I picked up the comb and started stroking it through his sweat-dampened hair.

He smelled like himself: like cinnamon and wood chips and clean cotton. The smell of wood chips was new since he'd started at the mill, but I liked it. If I asked, he told me about flipping logs or driving pallet loads around or flipping switches and doing safety checks. He told me about coffee break and who he sat with. And I tried to ask, but I forgot sometimes, just as I forgot the names of the men, his new friends, even as he was talking about them. I couldn't imagine his days. It was like he drove up the driveway every morning and vanished.

I combed his hair out on his warm skin and inhaled. He was so close and real. When I lifted the comb out, his hair curled around the knot at the top of his spine.

The blade of the scissors sliding against his skin made him shiver as I snipped a line across the nape of his neck. I brushed the cut hair from his back, lifted the hair up from the back of his head with the comb, and cut at an angle like I'd seen hairstylists do. His hair fell back to his head shorter, the cuts blending into the slight wave in his hair, my inexperience forgiven by the soft light and a natural curl.

Jazz Christmas standards slid out of the radio and time slowed. The fire crackled, the soup simmered, the smell of potatoes and pepper wafted around us. Danny sighed as I combed and cut his hair, complied when I moved his skull this way and that, moaned when I blew the loose hairs from the back of his neck. I straightened his head with my fingers and started on the hair around his ears.

"It's loud," he said. "It's like you're snipping right in my ear canal."

"I'm almost done."

"Don't rush. I like it." He snaked his arm around my waist and pulled me close.

"No touching," I said, but didn't mean it. I straddled his thigh as I moved to the front of his head. His eyes were closed, but he was smiling.

I used the nail scissors to cut his bangs. Little wisps of blond curls fell onto his jeans and stuck in his chest hair. I brushed them away with my fingertips. His breathing was audible and I was deliberate—leaning into him with a hip, pressing down with the hot flat of my hand to move him this way or that. The heat was rising in both of us. The kitchen felt like the only room on earth—the glint of light off the scissors blade, the smell of smoke from the fire. I nestled in between his legs as I cut, pausing, breathing near his ear. I could feel his hard cock against my thigh. He squeezed my hips, pulling me closer.

"Hold still." I laughed, and he was trying, but it was building in both of us: desire after a drought. I slid the comb into the thicket at his crown and combed the hair straight up and held it. I snipped. Hair slid down his face and tickled him. He sneezed, jerking free of my fingers. "Hey!"

He sneezed again. And again. He held his arm out, like wait, it'll stop, but it didn't. "I can't help it," he managed to pant between sneezes. They were violent. He bent at the waist with each one, his hair flopping forward, almost dry now. I waited, frustrated, and all the romance leaked out of the room.

I held myself still so the frustration wouldn't turn to fury, but it did. I couldn't stop it. I unravelled in the space of a second. "Forget it. I'm done." I put the comb down.

"Wait!" He sneezed. "Just a minute." He sneezed. Two more sneezes in quick succession. Piles of hair exploded with each blast of air. Hair blew all over the kitchen.

"I just cleaned this!"

He held his hands over his face and stood up. He held a finger out to me, just a minute, then rushed toward the bathroom, drifts of hair wafting in his wake. I poured myself another shot of whisky, drank it fast, and surveyed the damage. I grabbed my coat and left.

The cold was a relief after the heat of the cabin. I breathed in deep, felt the booze in my blood. I went to the shed first and grabbed a can of gas and a pack of matches. I followed the path down to the lake. The light spilling from the cabin windows was enough to show me the snow-trampled path and keep me from falling in the drifts.

I stopped on the path and looked back at the lit-up windows. We were like a movie in there. Every day, making coffee, cuddling the baby, and tonight: me cutting his hair, all framed like a TV screen. The haircut felt unreal already. The wind bit my cheeks. I tucked my face in my collar and tromped down the trail onto the ice, imagining Danny as I went, coming out of the bathroom, done sneezing, pink-cheeked and shorn. He'd see the room empty. He'd call my name, but not so loud he'd wake the baby. Seeing no sign of me, he'd look for my coat and boots, then he'd go to the window. Out on the dark lake he'd see a speck of fire—the flame from my match. He'd see me set it to the gas-dampened wood and he'd see the labour of his day go up in a whoosh of fire.

I found the bonfire pile in the dark. The wind tried to pull the can from my hand as I poured gas over the logs. I got most of it out, then I lit the match and dropped it on the wood. It went up just as I'd imagined—the whoomp of the gas-wet patch bursting into flame. I watched for a second, and then I unscrewed the nozzle and tipped the gas can up over the flames to get the last drops out. Fire lit the splash of gas, licked up the stream of droplets, and then the can was on fire. I threw it down, but my coat was on fire, too. I screamed. I shook my arms but the wind made it worse, flames crawling up my front to my face.

A weight hit me from behind and crushed me to the snow. I couldn't breathe. There was snow in my face, in my mouth. I wanted to scream, but all the air was gone. The fire roared beside my head. I was drowning. Something pummelled me and rolled me over. I looked up into Danny's face. Both of us were screaming, then we stopped, and he held me while I sobbed. His bare arms, goosebumps all over him. The bonfire caught deep inside the pile and whooshed higher. We stumbled away together, me holding tight to him, his hair golden and spiky in the firelight.

That night when he reached for me in bed I let him. I moved this way and that to make it sexier and more realistic. I moaned, I gasped. I gave him everything I had.

"More tea?" Rosie asked, solicitous and kind.

I blushed to have been caught thinking about sex and struggled to come back from so far away. "Thank you. Yes." And in answer to a question I'd only half heard, I said it again: "Yes, thank you. We had a nice Christmas. I was sure we'd been by since then."

CHORUS
Jill Stone, Arts Unlimited Building

Off the point, the rock breaks off and drops who knows how far into darkness. From above, the water changes from green to black, the limestone promise breaks, and underneath? Who knows what lies underneath. The jutting, rutted rock face of the point off Chance Bay, the one pierced through, is a beacon for boaters—they see the hole in the rock and they know they're almost home.

But come night, those rocks shift and move. The drop-off crawls closer to land, maybe to trick us into skinny-dipping when we're drunk. Some nights we don't go out. We sit onshore and watch the shifting colours off the point—green, blue, silver, gold. The sun sets right there, moving farther and farther south as the summer dies and the earth shifts.

Off the point, the rock drops off into rippling sand so far down the light only slips through in glimpses. And there—that's where the dead lay out hands of cards. Sons and fathers, brothers, uncles, cousins, sisters, mothers sit in a circle and lay down their hands, and their clothes drift off them with the current. The fish swim through their rib cages, and those of us onshore can't hear the slow-motion clacking of their bones knocking joint to joint.

Deep in this lake is a current that pulls the dead away from their quiet games, shifts the sand underneath them. Slowly, the lake drains down the river and the dead flow with the ancient river south to the Stuart, south to the Nechako, south to the Fraser, and then to the sea.

You'd believe it if you saw the cliff. If you saw the darkness where the swimmers don't swim, and if you get caught in the current, we'll find you over Sowchea way, or at the Stuart mouth, eyes wide open with weeds in your hair.

When the wind blows and the waves are so high a man might be swallowed whole, you can hear the thump in the rock tunnel, the waves shaking the point. Rumbles and groans. Why any man would choose that spot on that bay to live, no one knows—that drop-off looming, the river's pull. You know anybody out there will come to harm. That's what legend says. That's what they say in town.

RENEE

At five fifteen, Danny got home. I was waiting for him. He walked into the cabin with fogged glasses and I handed him the baby. After tea at Swannells', it'd been non-stop crying—mine and Tom's. Each of us too upset to even try to be okay.

"I'm going to yoga," I said, and walked back to the stove, leaving Danny still wearing his boots and coat in the foyer. I watched him while I stirred the chicken. He kissed the baby, then put him down among the shoes, where Thomas sat like a little Buddha and pulled a sandal to his mouth. Danny took the sandal and gave him a hat instead.

"Have you been to that before?"

"No. When would I?"

"Maybe while I was at work."

"How, Danny? You've got the car."

"Right. So, it's in town? How did you hear about it?"

"Oh, for God's sake! Yes, it's in town! I read about it in the paper and I'm taking the car and I'm going to town!" I slammed my fist down onto a dishtowel on the counter. I sucked in a breath, rubbed my face with the towel, then glared at him so he would know I wasn't sorry, that I was serious. I had my yoga pants on already.

"Go, Renee, by all means, go. We're not trying to keep you here." He picked up the baby. The wood stove rumbled in the corner. I saw Thomas look at his dad, then whack him in the face with his wide-open hand. Danny took Tom's hand in his and kissed it. I couldn't watch. All day I'd struggled to simply be. The baby, the crying, the cabin breathing all around us—I couldn't do it. Danny could. I hated him.

"He's fed. I should be a couple of hours at the most." Tears stopped up my throat. "Sorry I'm such a bitch."

Outside in the car, I was glad, for once, for the early dark. The hard part of getting out of the house was done and now I only had to drive to the high school and blend in. I gripped the steering wheel, eager but uneasy. I checked myself—my clothes were neutral, my hair slightly mussed like I hadn't given it too much thought. Perfect. I wondered how I would compare to the other mothers. I decided I would be casual, but not overeager; I would reveal myself slowly in conversation, leave them wanting a bit, curious about me. I smiled a little. As I neared the school, I breathed deep and tried to squash down my thoughts and worries.

In the fluorescent light of the school foyer, I could hear low music and voices coming from the gym. I walked down the hall, my purse in my hands, awkward and hyperaware. As I stopped to the side of the open double doors to take off my boots, I could hear women talking inside the gym.

"I wouldn't do it again if I couldn't have a midwife."

"I know. I couldn't have done it without mine."

"My husband was pretty good, but the doula was awesome. I'd have her babies if I could." The women laughed.

"Did you have a home birth?"

"Oh yeah, that was awesome, too. I couldn't stand the thought of the baby coming into the world in the hospital—it's so cold and sterile."

"I know. I was so happy to write 'successful home birth' in the baby book. I love my baby book, but it's hard to keep up with. Don't you find? All those blanks to fill in every day..."

I remembered labour like a battle I'd fought and lost. Twenty hours into it, with contractions two minutes apart and four centimetres away from full dilation, the foetal heart monitor flatlined. They wheeled me into an operating room at a run. Doctors and nurses yelled at one another—professionals with fearful eyes above their masks. Danny fell out of view.

I don't know what happened in those minutes of panic— I lay on my back, senseless from the scrubs down, breathing shakily through the oxygen mask while tears dripped into my ears. Finally, Danny's face came into sight again, his white mask crumpled and damp from crying. He talked to me and I heard his voice, a familiar murmur underneath the din of the operating theatre. Lights beat down on us in the cold room. Behind the screen of blankets across my chest, my body was wrenched back and forth as they pulled the baby out of the trap of my pelvis. I heard one doctor swear. Blood squirted across the chest of another. Danny talked and talked, stroking my hair, soothing me like an animal under his hand.

"It's a boy," someone said, and silence fell, and held, though the machines still beeped and something whooshed in the corner. "He's blue," the same voice said, and the noise ratcheted up again. Danny stopped talking and I closed my eyes. I was empty, exhausted. They didn't bring the baby to me; they resumed work on my body. The doctors sewed through layers and layers of skin. There was a hole in the room that a sound should have filled. A drip of fluid hammered the floor again and again. I squeezed my eyes shut and sobbed into my mask.

"Renee," Danny said. "Renee, Renee." I opened my eyes to him and swallowed him whole and we held each other, riveted together with the force of our stares. I threw my whole self into him and I felt him catch me. He touched my face. He kissed my temple through his paper mask. My body jostled back and forth, and then a thin, climbing voice squeaked out and grew to a wail from a corner of the room. Danny's eyes softened and flooded. We looked away from each other toward the sound, and Danny's hand dropped from my hair.

At the threshold of the high-school gym, I listened to the women say hospitals were for sick people, and that children ought to be born into loving arms in their family homes. I imagined Danny in our bedroom, the bed plastic-sheeted, smeared with blood and amniotic fluid, me, sprawled, dead, Thomas trapped inside me. I could see Danny, arms at his sides, open-mouthed and howling in our family home, and I knew that something may have been lost in Thomas's actual birth, but that the bloody tunnel of this imagined scene was worse. I turned away from the door, where inside the women were beginning to flow between the yoga mats set out on the floor. I put on my boots and walked away down the hall. The door banged shut behind me.

In the car, the heater blasted cold air at my face before it finally warmed. I followed the highway through the re-serve, over the bridge, and out of town. I flew past fields and sudden white stands of poplar and birch. The "Welcome to Fort St. James" sign rose up on the left and receded in the rear-view. The moon stabbed light down when the clouds shifted, illuminating sections of road, the corners of barns, stark fence posts held together by scraps of broken wire. I burned down the highway, furious and exultant, thinking I'd escaped—but from what? The women? The school? The willows in the ditch? I felt cowardly and wretched for not even giving it a try. Why hadn't I stayed? There was no way to know if all the women were the same. I remembered yoga classes in the city: my self-satisfaction at stretching and bending, being beautiful among beautiful strangers. I smacked the flat of my hand against the steering wheel.

It was like me to overreact. I wanted to close my eyes and scream. Instead, I pulled off the road and sat. There were no lights. There were no houses or barns or fences, just tight-packed pine forest a few metres from the highway. I leaned my head on the steering wheel and thought about going back to the cabin. Danny would have Thomas in bed, clean and fed. Maybe he'd have cracked himself a beer, or maybe made coffee.

I thought of him there in his grandpa's old cabin and felt worn out and wronged. I wanted a studio apartment in Kitsilano. I wanted to study at the Sorbonne. I wanted a body that hadn't known childbirth or anything but sun-drenched days and ease. I thought of Thomas, and guilt came seeping in, dark and wet. I wanted Thomas, but I wanted to want him more.

I started up the car and did a U-turn on the highway, barely looking around. There was more danger from passing wildlife than from turning blindly into the oncoming lane so late at night in this stalled season. I headed toward home, feeling like I was driving into a fog bank. The only thing that spurred me on were my breasts, which had started to fill, ready for the ten o'clock feeding.

Cow, I thought to myself, but I amended it to poor cow when tears sprang up. I cast around, eyes darting from thicket of bush to copse of trees, trying to think of something I could do instead of think, instead of feeling all this self-pity. My breasts stung and I landed on it: weaning the baby. I could do that. Eight months was long enough. It couldn't be that hard—I could buy formula tomorrow and start cutting out feedings. I had breastfeeding books to help me figure out how to do it. I wondered what Danny would think, but then I decided it was up to me, not him. I drove a little faster, following the lake out of town toward the bay, full to bursting with ideas of what I could do without having to sit down every few hours to feed the baby: I could put him in the playpen with a bottle while I drank a cup of tea without it going cold; I could finish the dishes or read a chapter without abandoning it halfway through. Thoughts roiled through me. I was on automatic pilot when I turned off the road into the parking lot of the pub.

I parked the car snug up to the Dream Beaver on the gravel and got out to stretch my legs. In the bright light of the street lamp the hulking Fords and flatbeds loomed. I was disoriented, surprised to find myself there. A throaty laugh came from behind me and I turned toward the sound.

Glory grinned at me from the gloom beside the building. "Didn't expect I'd see you quite so soon." She dropped her cigarette butt and ground it out with her heel. She gestured to the pub. "Don't look like much, but it's mine. I think they pay the mortgage with my tab alone." She snorted. "Come on in!" She held out her hand toward the massive carved front doors of the bar.

Two beavers, nose to nose, met at the crack between the doors. Their cross-hatched tails were grotesquely exaggerated, stretching twice the length of the beavers to the height of the door frame. Raised, inlaid silver teeth protruded from their mouths. I stared a second and ran my hand over the left beaver's head.

"Nice."

"A bit fucking elaborate, if you ask me." Glory pushed past me to haul one door open. A fug of smoke and nighttime bodies wafted out, and she took my hand as we walked in.

The pub was new to me, but the feel of it, the cloying smoke and heat reminded me of all the bars I'd known. The bar itself stretched a good three metres into the centre of a wide room whose recesses, the walls, and all the alcoves were decorated with bright-eyed stuffed owls, fish, beavers, and an enormous buffalo head. Glory led me to the far end of it, and leaned over it to shout at a burly woman who was glaring at us.

"Hi, Sandy. Two Canterbury. No glasses."

Sandy didn't quit glaring. She glared while her hands grabbed two bottle necks sticking out of the ice in the sink. She plunked them on the bar, then set two glasses beside the brown bottles. "Six bucks, Glory."

"I said no glasses."

"Whatever."

"Put it on my tab."

Sandy looked like she had more to say. The red bulbs in the light fixtures above her head made the streaks in her hair violently purple. As she turned away, I distinctly heard her utter the word "whore." I looked at Glory, who smiled out at the room in general.

The room was full, mostly of men. Glory looked like she'd come home after a long day of work. She took my hand and pulled me toward a table.

"We'll sit with Bill."

Bill's belly rested on his thighs. He wore spiked boots that were unlaced so the tall sides of them slouched along his calves. He reached out and caught Glory's skirt. "Hey, sugar lady."

"Hey, yourself." She sat beside him in a leather chair. She pushed me toward another chair and put her feet on Bill's lap. "Hold these for me, would you?"

The table erupted in laughter. Glory's skirt fell down from her waist in a curtain, suggesting the long bare legs behind the fabric. The men seemed all mouth and suspenders and whiskers to me. I sat as compactly as I could in the chair Glory offered—the arms had a sticky film I didn't want to touch.

"Who's yer friend, Glory?" Bill looked me up and down.

"This is Renee. She's new," Glory told him. "Renee's on the prowl."

"I am not," I burst out.

Glory looked at Bill's cigarette, then at his face, raising her eyebrows. He leaned over and put a cigarette in her mouth, then lit it and sat back. She inhaled, then exhaled, sizing me up. "Well, maybe she's not."

The men laughed and the table shook. I sat, small in my chair, my purse on my lap. A man with a skinny face shadowed by a ball cap leaned toward me. I tried not to recoil.

"Don't sweat it, little girl. She don't mean no harm."

I looked at Glory, stretched out like a panther on a tree limb, blowing smoke up toward the bison head above her. "I guess not."

"Drink yer beer. You'll be alright."

Two beers later, I was drunk. I used the length of the bar to find my way to the bathroom. The place was packed. Men and a few women sat crammed together on the benches and chairs. I took three steps and pushed my arm in between two men to grip the bar so I didn't fall. One of the men spun around suddenly and knocked my knees out from under me. I fell in his lap, facing the bar, and my eyes landed on a plaque embedded in the wood in front of me.

"Whoa, lady," he said, and picked me up by the elbows to right me. My eyes were still crossed from trying to read the plaque. This cracked him up. "Look at her eyes, Brad!"

"Jesus, how many drinks have you had?" Brad had a crooked grin. His short hair and beard made him look more deliberately scruffy than Bill and his friends. These two men had all their teeth, and I could smell aftershave or deodorant through their flannel shirts.

"Just two...or three...I think. Prob'ly not four..."

They smirked and kept me at the bar with the angles

their legs made, their feet propped up on the stool legs.

"You don't know? " Brad looked down at me from under blond lashes.

"I'm not used to it." I felt compelled to explain. "I'm nursing, so I don't drink much." All three of us looked at my breasts just as wet flowers blossomed over the nipples. "Oh shit," I said, bringing both hands up to cover the leaks.

The men's eyes went wide, and I knew this was something they'd never seen before. Under my horror I almost felt smug, like I'd pulled back a curtain, but shame seeped in fast and I pushed through their knees, fumbling for the sanctity of a toilet stall.

When Glory came into the bathroom, she found me turning my T-shirt around so the stains were on the back. My sports bra was next to the sink.

"I guess you sprung a leak. You didn't mention you were still breastfeeding that baby."

"Didn't come up," I mumbled, struggling to find the armholes in my shirt.

"Doesn't matter. No one cares. Hey, are you having fun?" She pushed up close and sat on the counter.

I considered my options: I wasn't having fun, so I could leave right now, go back to the bay and Danny and the tomorrows just like all the yesterdays, or I could stick this night out and see where it took me. "I should probably go home."

"Why? We just got here."

"I've got the baby at home and I've never left him before..."

"Jesus, it's good you came out then, you deserve it. How old is he?"

"Eight months."

"Christ! That's a long time to be at home without going crazy! I was out a week after having my kid."

"You've got a kid?"

Glory grimaced. She busied herself adjusting her clothes. "Yeah." She stared at me. "But we're not here to talk about kids, are we? We're here to have fun. That's why I'm here, you know, to make sure you have fun. That's why we met. I think it was destiny." She raised her arms above her head in a flourish and flicked her hair back. I laughed and listed a bit to the left.

"Hey, what's that plaque on the bar?" I asked, shrugging back into my hooded sweatshirt and tucking my bra into one of the pockets.

"That's Smokey's. He died last year on the lake. Stupid fuck." Glory turned to fix her hair in the mirror. She pushed it back from her face, but small curls sprung round to frame it in the damp of the bathroom. She was gorgeous. I couldn't not look at her.

She took a lipstick out of her pocket and touched the end of it to the mirror, stroking a lascivious gash of colour through her face.

"Smokey," she said, softly, while she drew. "He left me massive tips. I might have fucked him once in the grass out back, but he was a sorry, fat man with nothing besides his his boat. Didn't surprise me when he died. Didn't surprise anyone. Miss him like a bastard, though." She turned her head to meet my eyes in the mirror. "I wrote a song about it. You wanna hear? I'll add it to our set."

The bathroom door banged shut behind her. I glanced back at myself in the mirror. In red, where Glory had been, a crude broken heart marred the mirror. My cheeks were scarlet and my eyes were glassy.

When I emerged from the bathroom, Glory was standing on a small stage under a stuffed eagle. She pulled her sweater over her head, and sloughed it off like a too-big, second skin. She reached for her guitar. Everyone's eyes were on her. As she strapped on the guitar, I noticed movement among the tables in the far recesses of the pub. A woman, taller and sturdier than she was, but feline in the same way, wove between the tables toward the stage. Crystal stepped onto the stage and picked up a banjo. Their eyes met once, and I saw Glory's lips move. Then Glory turned to the crowd. The first notes on the guitar were a plank her voice dove off.

> There's a bar stool at Edna's
> with a name on a plaque
> of a lake-faring bastard
> with a giant's own laugh.
> I'd buy your first pint
> if you walked through the door,
> but we don't have to laugh
> at your jokes anymore.

Crystal's banjo leapt in to hold up Glory's voice, and then suddenly, with a frisson of discord, her voice slid in underneath Glory's. The banjo filled out the sound until it flooded the room. The way their voices held the notes, the way they glanced darts at one another, the way their voices twined like two silver cords, made my ears throb, and left an aching hole in my chest when they stopped singing. The chorus almost did me in. There was a deliberate fuck-you in the plainness of their music I'd never heard before.

> Smokey, your laugh rolled right up to the roof.
> It fell down on us sinners like god's living proof.
> You had faith in your barmaid and I don't know why
> but I loved you for laughing, you old, fat, hard-living dear,
> of a laughing loud bastard, of a kind-hearted guy.

There's a bar stool at Edna's
with a letter-pressed plaque
for a lake-faring bastard
with a giant's own laugh,
and though it's a stool
with a helluva view,
no one sits there, Smokey,
'cause we save it for you.

"So, get the fuck off his stool, you pussy!" Glory yelled
from the stage, and pointed to the men who'd laughed at
me earlier. Brad was surprised and chuckled nervously, but
when the crowd turned to him and rumbled in agreement,
he and his pal paid for their beers and left. "That's right,"
Glory said, and pranged the guitar. "Now let's rock out!" The
crowd laughed and she strummed fast and wild, her hair all
over the place. Crystal propped her banjo against the leg of a
stool and lit a cigarette. She left it burning in an ashtray while
she signalled the bartender for a drink. Glory settled into another song. Their voices rose like angels wrestling mid-flight,
feathers flying everywhere, unsettling and divine.

I leaned on the wall with my fists balled against my legs,
so full of want I felt nauseous. It wasn't the songs I wanted.
It wasn't the beer, or the night out. Was it Glory? I didn't
know. I felt numb and alone at the back of the room. I
glanced at a clock with a bikini model in it. Twelve thirty.
The drunk hum in my head helped suppress thoughts of
Danny and Thomas. I slumped down the wall until I sat on
the floor. I watched Glory play and I sucked the sight and
sound into me as tight as I could so the rest of the bar didn't
exist, just Glory, her ragged voice and wild hair, the poten-
tial of her friendship.

CHORUS
Bill Bowmann, Dream Beaver Pub

I'll tell you about this lake. It's a man-eater. Eats its fill, leaves the rest of us to tell about it. You'd believe it, you watch those storms come down the lake. It's not even as big as some lakes, but it's a killer.

First thing they teach you when you're a baby: "You're on the water when the water goes black, you get off, quicker'n quick." I told my own kids that, and they told theirs. Someone should tell the newcomers, too.

While back, some fella from out east comes here for the fishing. And it's good fishing, too—people been making their living off fishing here for a long time. He comes out here and tries his luck. Doesn't have any the first day, so he rents a boat from me. Doesn't have any the second day, neither, so he rents a bigger boat. Guys hanging around at the wharf say, "You gotta get a local to show you the good spots," but this fella's a big-shot fisherman, doesn't need anybody to show him around. Goes out the third day and doesn't come back. No sign of the boat, neither. Like someone just reached down and plucked them both up. His truck sat out front for a long time. Got it towed eventually.

This lake is full of fools. Fools who wouldn't listen. Fools who thought they could outrun a storm or outlast the water. Drunk fools. Dead fools.

The worst thing I ever heard was about those two kids that winter. When the ice is on the lake, and everyone's out on their snow machines ripping around, I remember.

Everyone remembers. It was just after Christmas. Those kids were party-hopping along the north shore, bonfire to bonfire, gunning their snow machines, racing. It was some bad winter—warm and then freezing cold—no one drove their trucks out on the ice that year. Those kids. They were in love. They were the kids you heard about even if you had no kids and didn't care for teenagers. Those two, I picture them like Romeo and Juliet. Her hair whipping around, her arms holding him tight. Them taking off from the others.

Funny thing is, I always picture them flying, not falling, not sinking, or drowning, but like there was a cliff in the middle of the lake and they just drove off it. Disappeared into the stars.

I hate that story, but it stays with me. I went out with the search parties over New Year's, but then I gave up. Didn't want to find them. Rather picture her smiling into his back and the rumble of the snow machine underneath them, the two of them ripping up the clouds.

I been living on this lake longer'n anyone, almost. I watch the storms come down from Portage beat the living shit out of my shore, bend the trees in half, break my windows, sometimes. I respect this lake. I don't ice-fish no more. I barely fish at all. I don't go out if the sky looks weird, and sure as hell, if the water goes black, I head for shore. Batten down the hatches.

RENEE

It was almost one o'clock when Glory grabbed me by the wrist and pulled me behind the bar. "Out here!" she whispered, and we ran past the beer cooler, out a back door, and onto the deck.

We stood near the wall beside a barbecue and Glory lit a cigarette. I struggled to get my hoodie over my head without strangling myself. "Is this normal?"

"What? No, it's backward."

"Not my shirt—the night."

She shrugged. "It's how it is. Well, tonight's a good night, I guess. No fights so far, no blood, no ambulance. No jealous girlfriends, no knives, no trucks smashed up in the ditch, yet. So yeah, it's a good night. But it's not always like this. Last week the kitchen caught fire."

"Really?"

"It wasn't so bad. They put it out fast, but kept the place shut down. No chips for a whole night!" I watched her to see if she was joking. She sucked at her cigarette and spit tobacco out at the wind. "Yeah, it's a funny place, but it's homey."

"But what are we doing here?"

"We're hiding."

"Yes, I caught that, but who are we hiding from?"

"From all those jerks waiting out front to give us a ride. If you look you'll see at least three trucks and maybe a car. Bill's is the biggest truck. He'll give up in a minute or two and the rest will follow."

"Don't we want a ride, though?"

"Not with those drunks."

I leaned against the wall. Maybe we were the drunks. My head was spinning.

She finished her cigarette, said, "Listen," and held up her hand. A truck started up and impatiently revved its engine. Then it rumbled off. In quick succession two more ignitions lit, then revved, then rolled off, getting quieter in the distance.

"Alright then. Shall we?" She held out her elbow like a gentleman. I took it and followed her off the deck and into the forest behind the pub. The willows grew thick near the shore and the lake sounded loud and wet—the wind was coming up. She steered us onto a path.

"Where are we going?" I asked, after some time walking.

"To the Cabaret. It's just like the pub but it's got a fancy name."

"Won't all those men be there, too?"

"Of course they will."

"But won't they be mad?"

"Who cares? They wait until I get there and then the party starts again." We walked on in silence, bumping hips, stumbling occasionally. Ahead, I could just make out the jetty at Cottonwood Beach. I had passed it so many times in daylight, wishing I was one of the people lazing about in their swimsuits, so casual and self-contained. Now the jetty looked slick and secret, like a meeting place for lovers looking to keep things quiet.

We walked awhile in silence, then Glory said, "I didn't tell the truth back there." Her voice startled a nervous laugh from me. I stopped when she didn't join in. "I never fucked Smokey. I just said I did. I don't know why. Once we went back behind the pub after closing and he held me around the waist and cried. I let him. He kneeled with his fat face in my waist and I could smell his greasy hair. Then I drove him home in his truck and parked it beside his shop. I don't even know why he was crying. He'd fallen asleep in the passenger seat, so I just left him there and walked home. I never fucked him. Everyone thinks I did, but I didn't. He was just a soft, sloppy old man with a beauty boat, until that boat washed up in Whitefish Bay half-full of water and rotting fish, and no Smokey. No one knows what happened to him and nobody talks about him anymore."

We stood there breathing.

"I wish I knew what to say."

"Don't say anything." She took me by the arm again and led me toward the dirty lights of town. "Just watch your feet."

I stopped after a moment. "Glory, listen. I've got to go. I can't be out here, I've got a baby at home and he hasn't eaten." Unease had built to panic, despite the booze, and I wanted to run.

"What are you talking about? Isn't your man at home?"

"Yes, my 'man' is at home, but he hasn't got boobs, has he?"

"You tell me." Glory laughed.

"I'm serious. I need to go back."

"You can go back, but I wouldn't wanna walk through these woods if I didn't know the way." She dropped my arm.

"Don't do that! Glory, show me the way!"

"Can't. I've got a date."

"With who?"

"Whom."

"What?"

"With whom have you got a date, is correct."

"What do you care about grammar!"

"Now I know what you think of me." She was gone in the dark.

"Wait a minute, I didn't mean it, Glory..." I stumbled, reaching for her. A lighter zipped, then flared, and she was visible sucking at the filter of a cigarette. She inhaled and let her thumb off the tab. The light disappeared.

"Sit down, mama. Don't stress yourself out."

I sat down next to her on a rock, shaky and sick.

"You just don't know what to think, do you? Here, I'll tell you what I see and then you tell me if I'm wrong." She patted my arm. "You move up here with your sweetheart and your baby. You think it's gonna be a better life—fresh start, perfect. But. You get up here and there's one grocery store. One cop shop. One liquor store and no Starbucks. You start to get scared. Then your hubby goes to work, and it's just you and the baby, and what the hell are you supposed to do with your mind?"

I sucked in air and held it. Tears stung my eyes.

Glory patted my arm. "Don't worry. It's like that for almost everyone. That's why I gave mine up—couldn't do it, didn't want to try. I know what they say about me, but I don't care. It's tough shit, being a mom. It's inconsistent with my desires."

I laughed through tears. "You don't make sense. You're all shit and what the fuck and then whom and inconsistent with my desires." I sniffed and wiped my nose on my sleeve. "I don't know what I'm doing here, Glory."

"You want me to tell you that, too?"

"I don't know. You're the first person I've talked to since the fall."

"Really? That's a long time."

"Well, not quite. I guess I talk to Danny and Thomas. And the gas station attendant." I could smell the lakeshore. "Where are we? What does this place look like in daylight?"

"Not much. There's a runoff drain lets out around here somewhere, so there's garbage and weeds. That's what you smell—that and secret love affairs. People come down here to fuck."

"Here? Yuck."

"Don't be so high and mighty—not every love affair is roses and sunshine. Some are stuck with chip bags and mud."

I laughed, but something struck me. "Glory, where's your baby?"

"She's not a baby anymore. She's ten."

"You know that's not what I meant."

"Fine. You wanna know? I gave her away right after she was born. It was the best thing. For everyone. Fuck. I don't want to talk about it."

"How is it best for everyone? I mean, I can see it's good for you because you don't want to be a mom and you've got your career, but how did you get pregnant in the first place? Who was the dad? Someone you know, I guess..." I petered out.

"Oh, fuck off. You're gonna judge me just like everyone else. Go ahead. Judge! It's not like I haven't heard it before. Let me list everything they call me: whore, for one. Witch, bitch, selfish, fucked up, drunk, unfit, selfish. Oh, I said that already? How about Jezebel? How about slut? How about everyone's worst nightmare. Fucksake. It's not like I killed anyone. I made a lot of people happy, in fact."

I shook my head. "How?"

"You wouldn't understand. Never mind. Let's get out of here." She stood, but she didn't go anywhere. I could see her outline, now that my eyes were used to the dark. She stood with her hands loose at her side, her head down. "You don't get to choose who you're going to be, here. You can try, but it's not up to you."

"What do you mean?"

"You can say you're anything you want, but it's others

who decide for you." She clapped her hands.

I looked around. "Where's Crystal? Did you tell me already?"

Her voice lost its smile. "Don't know. Don't care."

I mumbled an apology.

"Never mind. She's just mad at me. She went home. But who needs her? The whole night is ahead of us!"

I stood and let her lead me up from the woods. I was thinking about what she'd said, feeling it out, because it sounded significant to me, especially after the day and night I'd had. I was drunk, I knew, but—what if you made what other people might think was a selfish decision, and it was actually the best decision for everyone? I wanted to live in the space around that thought for a while. I started to feel my way toward an idea.

CHORUS
Jim Swannell, deck chair, Chance Bay

I'd been brushing the low trailhead near Pope Mountain one of the first decent days this spring when I seen her with the baby in the pack hiking up toward the lookout. I'll tell you now, I followed her, but I don't feel bad about it—I seen her eyes the last time she stopped in for tea with me and the missus. Bruises, they were. Dark brown bruises for eyes, with no hope in them at all.

I trailed 'em up to the top and then I hailed her. Didn't want to startle her but I did all the same. She got all shifty but stayed polite. I stood with her there, and breathed in the morning. Perfect day. We could see clear out to South-side across the lake. I says, nice day for it, and she nods some. Pushes her hair behind her ear. I can't say why I told her all I did, except I could see she was struggling. Like a moose in sink mud—she was all agangle in it, stuck, like she couldn't tell why the dirt was suddenly swallowing her when yesterday it was solid.

Listen, I says to her. The walls close in after a while. I says, that cabin was good for Roy and Catherine, but it's mighty small for a growing family. It's good to get out after a long winter. Not the worst winter, but it probably felt that way to her. The first is always the worst.

I told her the bay's been called a lot of things over the years, Hard Luck Bay and Bad Luck Bay and Home Place Bay, and now they just call it Northside. But you know what it used to be—used to call it Chance Bay. For Roy Chance.

The French down at Dog Creek called him *chanseux* because he was—had the best spot on the lake.

She kept polite, like you should be to an old coot, but I needed to tell her something. I says, listen, wife of Danny Chance, it's a choose-yer-own-adventure world. I read those choose-yer-own-adventure books for kids where you get a number of different choices for an ending. If you pick right, you get a happy ending right off, but if you don't, you pick over and over again until you get it right. I never expect to get it right the first time. I guess I have the right to choose again. Every day you choose. You choose your pants and shirt, you choose the trail you'll take, and you choose your own moral way, every single day. And I'm not saying it's always got to be the high road, neither. Look here, I says to her, this trail brought us up to a view, but if we took this path every day we wouldn't notice the view anymore. Most times we're just getting for getting's sake. Today we're stopping to take a look. And that counts for something.

She stays quiet for a bit and we listened to the birds and the baby snoozed in the pack, but I could see her thinking. She's shaking some, trying not to cry, and I don't know what to do, dammit. Didn't mean to make her cry. But she's got fortitude. She pulls herself together and, just like I said nothing at all, she says, who built this trail. Well, that pleased me. I got to tell her I did. I followed a deer trail and brushed it out, so I'd have somewhere to walk and think. I says, I didn't know others would get so much pleasure out of it or I'd have done it years ago.

She thanks me, for what, I don't know—the trail, the conversation—but she's done, I can tell you that. She shrugs her pack more comfy, bids me good morning, and off she goes, back down into the mud bog of her mind.

RENEE

It was past time to go home: my breasts were swollen under my T-shirt, so taut they didn't jiggle despite my bra being in my pocket. I pretended the sick feeling in my gut was due to mixing alcohol—I'd had beer, a cooler, some yellow drink Glory gave me, and now I found myself with a gin and tonic in one hand and a rum and Coke in the other. I wasn't sure if either was mine, but I knew, if I was honest with myself, that the nausea was at least partly guilt.

The inside of the Cabaret was more dank, more smoky, and more full of propped-up drinkers than the pub. Music pumped from speakers stacked on either side of a glassed-in booth, where a man with headphones and a cigarette hanging out of his mouth alternately groped a control board and a number of women stuffed into the booth with him. The music felt so thick I imagined I could see it, a grey, pulsing aura surrounding each person, but I knew the smoke was from burning tobacco and the haze was due to fatigue. Thomas had allowed only two-hour stretches of sleep between feeds last night, and the thought of him made me need to throw up. I beelined for the washroom. Glory didn't seem to notice.

In a washroom stall, I leaned against the metal door and contemplated the toilet. I had to pee but there was no seat. I also thought I might puke, but there was no way I was going to kneel on the wet floor. Hair and foam floated past my feet in the black, oily slick around the base of the toilet. I placed my feet on drier spots and waited for the bile to sub-side. After a minute, I managed to roll up my yoga pants and squat over the toilet with my hands braced on the sides of the stall, whose walls were strangely high. I worried my butt would show, and the women lined up outside by the counter, who were yelling in one another's ears and passing a joint, would laugh. I waited to pee, trying to relax enough to let it flow, but not so much that I'd release my grip on the walls and fall in the toilet. The stall next door banged open and a woman fell to her knees inside it. She leaned back on her haunches, shimmied a packet out of her tight white jeans and lay out a line of cocaine on a dry spot on the floor. I gaped as she plugged one nostril and leaned forward, the curtain of her hair closing around her.

Finally, my bladder released. When I emerged from the stall, I found the bathroom empty. There was a hole in the vanity where a sink should have been, but someone had kindly written directions on the mirror to spit on your hands and wipe them on your pants. I could barely see myself through the black ink that marked the mirror with advice: *They call us cokc-sukers but that's all they want! Annie John is a ho and a bad lay! Glory you cunt you better watch ur back!!!*

Out on the dance floor, Glory danced with a woman to a song with the refrain "Honk honky tonk woman." I moved in close to her, trying to lay a claim, but she danced on, oblivious to me, a little smile on her lips, her eyelids at half-mast. A man danced near her who was at least a foot taller than everyone else. He stared at my breasts with approval. I closed my eyes to shut him out and let the music move me. It was so rare and good to feel okay inside my head with my eyes closed; I felt invisible and free, and far away.

I felt hands on my waist and automatically swayed toward the warm palms tight on my hips. I opened my eyes and saw the tall man staring intently at me, rubbing his hands up my sides and back down to rest on the bones of my hips. My instinct was to recoil—I'd thought he was Glory, but when he saw that fear flicker in my eyes, he gripped me tighter, leaned in, and yelled in my ear. I couldn't understand what he'd said, so I shook my head and furrowed my brow at him.

"You move like water!" he shouted. He took his hands from my hips and placed them on either side of my face. His lips brushed my ear and I could smell his body. Panic welled in me. He yelled in my ear: "You are such a sexy dancer!"

I wasn't. I knew how I looked in yoga pants and a soiled T-shirt. I'd had men come on to me before, but even as my heart raced and I pulled away, I was falling for it. His hot hands cupped my face in a way Danny never did. It wasn't a thing Danny would do, and until now, it wasn't something I'd known I'd like. The man looked directly into my eyes, and even though I knew he was on the make, I smiled a new smile, a Glory half-smile, a sideways smirk, looking right back into his eyes with confidence born out of his attention.

"There's a party after." He pulled me close by the damp back of my neck. I couldn't get over his being so casual with my body; no stranger had ever drawn me near like this. "You should come. You're coming with me." He smiled at me and his long lashes flapped over dark eyes. Someone smacked my bum. I whipped around and it was Glory, her arm around a dark-skinned woman in white pants.

She leaned in. "You're not falling for this, are you?"

"No." I blushed, dancing out of her reach. I looked back at the man, who was miming something vigorous and mysterious at the DJ. Glory pulled my hand.

"Not him," she said, right in my ear. She was serious. "Don't. You'll regret it."

Alarm zinged through my chest. I looked back at the tall man, his skinny legs swathed in tight black acid-washed jeans, the lights from the booth flashing purple and white.

"Glory." I turned, but she was gone and the man had a hand on my wrist. I shook my arm hard and slipped his grip. The crowd jumped up and down to a new song. I pushed through them. The room changed—the walls seemed farther apart and bodies heaved and throbbed in the corners. I shoved my way through the dancers, into the hall, and this, too, seemed different—it stretched long and white before me. I didn't remember coming in this way. Two women with red lips reared up suddenly, very near. I pressed myself against the wall, squeezed past their bare arms and midriffs, and ran. A big man stood with his arms crossed, staring out a glass door. He turned when he heard my slapping feet and panting breath.

"Hey, lady!" He reached for me, but I was too quick and dodged his reach. I slammed into the door and it swung easily, pitching me out in the parking lot. I skidded to a halt on my hands and knees.

"Well, howdy," Glory said, around a breath of smoke.

She startled me and I flinched. How had she gotten outside so fast? I pressed my skinned palms into my pants. The night felt high and empty, like the sky was receding or a camera was panning out to leave me a dirty speck in a dirt parking lot. "I'm going home."

"Yeah? How? You gonna fly?" She laughed.

I said nothing. We were quiet while she smoked, and I struggled against gravity to stand.

"Go, then," she said, finally. She ground out her smoke and looked carefully at me. "If you're going, go. Don't stay here if you don't want to get caught up in it. But you better go now. The bar's gonna close in ten minutes and this parking lot will be a zoo."

"Glory." My voice buzzed, uncertain of its register.

"God, Renee. You don't know when to listen."

"I don't know what to listen to! Or who! I don't know if I can trust you or me or..." I lurched toward her.

"Go home, little girl. Figure out what you want before you come back here looking for me."

"I'm not looking for you. Jesus!"

"You won't find Jesus here."

"Shut up!"

"Get out of here. I'm serious."

"That's what I'm trying to do! I hate it here! I hate this place! I'm *trying* to get out of here!"

She looked evenly at me. "Fine. Let's go, then. Seriously. Let's go to Vancouver. We can leave together."

"What?" I tried to keep her still, to follow what she was saying.

"Let's go. If you want to go so much, let's do it."

"But, what about..."

"Look, if you're so unhappy, let's do something about it. I want to get out of here, too. We're a good team. We'll just leave and start new. Vancouver. We can be there before suppertime tomorrow."

I stared at her with confusion. Hope bloomed in me. "Really?"

"Sure. It'll be great."

I reeled, rocking back on my heels.

"You get the car and I'll get my bag and we'll meet at the boarded-up gas station in an hour, okay?" Glory held me by both arms. She spun me around until I faced the parking lot exit and gave me a little push. "That's the way."

I recognized the main street once I started walking. I could feel the slow drop of the road down toward the lake, a great big emptiness pulling me to the shore. I walked and kept walking, and it would be easy to leave, I realized. I just needed to keep moving. I felt led by a string, so that I was free to watch the water coming into focus, into individual waves, then into only one wave making and remaking itself, the barest flicker of white at its tip.

Out of town the street lights were sporadic, and once the sidewalk ended, the lights ended, too. I kept the empty hollow of the lake on my left. Eventually, I moved to the road's centre line, only able to see silver outlines on trees and rocks. There were cracks in the asphalt—wide, sharp-edged craters created by the frost as it thawed and eased out of the road. I tried to avoid them. The potholes were darker patches on the dark road, but I couldn't tell if they were ice skiffs or actual holes. I picked myself out of five before I reached the pub.

The parking lot was empty except for our car. I considered my options: leave it and walk back to the house, or drive. My legs prickled where the skin was scraped raw from my falls. The hood of the car shone with ice.

I dug the keys out of my hoodie pocket, unlocked the car, and climbed in. It felt so good to melt into the seat and to smell the familiar fusty air. I turned the key in the ignition and peered out the windshield, squinting to see if the fog was on my eyes or on the glass.

I pulled out slowly. Neat piles of downed branches and massive jumbles of trees and brush stood ready to burn at the roadside. I drove past the old church and its graveyard with the tippy wooden fences, past hectares of woods and bush and trees. I drove, lost in the hum of the motor and the jangle of my own breathing. It felt like a canvas of the night was rigged on a roller flowing past, the stars on a wheel above me, spinning in place.

What would happen if I left? I wondered. To Thomas and to Danny? The thought of the baby brought my milk ducts buzzing to life again, and a new surge of wet seeped through my shirt. Damn, I thought, and tears sprang forth, too, dripping down my face. My nose ran. I hadn't meant for this— I'd just been after a yoga class, maybe tea with new friends, mothers, too, who understood my whirling emotions. I hadn't intended to be alone in the night, lactating uselessly, my husband scared for my whereabouts. I wondered whether Danny had called the cops. What would he say to them? And what about Thomas? We had formula, but had he taken a bottle? I was an awful mother. I cried and hiccupped.

Eventually, I rattled up to the driveway. I took my foot off the gas and coasted until the car stalled and stopped. I stared out the windshield and saw my own porch light shining through the trees. I was soaked and shaken, close enough to call out to my husband, but I didn't. I opened the car door, careful not to slam it closed. It barely caught. I leaned against the cool metal and watched the house. No inside lights, no movement.

I got my legs working and stumped up the driveway. When I was close enough, I could see Danny asleep in a chair. The fire was out. He looked cold, huddled up in his clothes, white-faced and rumpled and drawn. I should open the door, I knew, but I hesitated. I shouldn't smell like smoke and beer. I should have been home before morning, but the light was creeping out of the lake, leaking over the water, giving individual facets to each wave. I listened to the rocks rattle in the bay and watched my husband sleep. How could I leave? I thought of Glory, standing outside the gas station waiting for me, of more blank days, of winters like the endless winter I'd just passed. How could I stay?

CHORUS

Dr. Allan Albright, Classico Coffee and Tea,
downtown Fort St. James

All through the winter, the ice makes its dissatisfaction known. It groans and cries, grinds itself into itself. It shifts and cracks, unreliable and ruthless. There were winters we used it as an ice road from town to Pinchi and Tache, bringing provisions to those reserve towns and doctoring there. Those years the ice was better than the highway; it was a smooth, wide-open highway across miles of frozen water, fish underneath you, wondering at the vibrations of tires, I guessed. I thought about that while I drove.

But it rots, you see, and you can't know when it will happen. You hear stories. We saw an ice house swallowed overnight, stovepipe and all. We woke in the morning to smooth snow covering the surface, the fishing hut gone. We weren't sorry—there had been parties in that hut all winter: ice-fishing parties with fireworks and booze. Sarah and I watched from the porch. They drove down our driveway like it was a public access onto the lake and parked behind the ice house. We didn't call the police out of fear of retaliation. We weren't sorry when the lake ate it whole.

Thirty years we've been in this house on this bay and every year the snow is different, the ice is different, but the winter always feels interminable. Because it never thaws the same way twice, you can't tell if the ice will be off in April or in June. Some Februaries were so mild I was fooled into planting, but then the snows came again and the spring was harsher than ever. Sarah always says don't fuss, that spring will come, but I'm never sure. The years the weather is late in breaking, my patients come in with burns, cuts, bruises—domestic abuse and, in my opinion, the results of unbearable pining for open water, frost-free days. I see people wound tighter and tighter over the winter, and when the sun finally melts the dirty snowdrifts in town, I don't see anyone anymore. Business drops off to nothing when it thaws.

February through May make me want to pack up and leave. We consider it, Sarah and I, and if it weren't for her illness, we would travel more to make living here more bearable. I think about retiring to Grand Cayman. I think about sea turtles and a warm breeze, not the freezing gale off this godforsaken lake all winter long. I wouldn't look back, but Sarah would. I read an account in her weather journal of the ice coming off in the spring of 1978 that rivals a poem; crystal, she wrote, and columns and tinkling, and when I read it, I could see our lakeshore in my mind, the black hole of open water beyond the ice, the ringing chimes of ice spikes succumbing to lapping tongues of water. She loves this place.

I tend the wounded and the ill, the men and women and children who populate this place at the end of the highway, and sometimes I can't see for all the hard cases and the cracks in the skin of my hands. Sarah sees the water, the lake nibbling its own shore, and knows its beauty. Will we leave here? No. She never will, and I couldn't sleep without my wife at my side or, truth be told, the sound of the waves on this shore.

RENEE

Thomas gurgled and sang in his cot when the heat made it through the blackout curtain over his window. It was too early. I waited to see how long it would take him to get from singing to yelling his head off. He yelped to see if that would rouse us, and my eyes flickered open.

"Hey," Danny said in a soft voice.

I waited a second. Then said: "What?" I didn't have anything for him: kindness, patience. I could give him nothing.

"Are you alright?"

"Compared to what?"

Danny lay back on his pillow as if defeated. I rose up on an elbow and faced him.

"What?" I asked again, but I didn't care to know.

He stared out the window, then seemed to decide to be direct. "Where were you? Ren, you were gone all night. I thought you might be dead."

"Obviously, I'm not."

He turned to me. "What is with you? We don't talk except to fight. You stay out all night, and you don't think it's worth talking about?"

Thomas squawked and we heard him thumping the bars of his crib with his feet. I tossed off the covers. I rose, naked, and left the room.

Danny yelled from the bedroom, "Renee, talk to me! Don't walk away!"

"Lower your voice." I came back into the room with Thomas in my arms. He was delighted to see his dad, yelling and flapping his arms, squirming to get down. I set him on the bed and he lunged to clamber all over Danny and pressed his open mouth onto Danny's cheek in a kiss.

"Hi, son." Danny was distracted from the conversation, as I meant him to be. Thomas crawled toward the edge of the bed. Danny grabbed him as he leapt for the carpet and leaned over farther to set him on the floor safely. "Something happened last night. I can tell. Tell me."

I stood at the full-length mirror, pushing my arms through the sleeves of my housecoat, watching my own face.

"Renee," Danny tried again, "I thought you were dead." I turned to him then. "I thought I'd never see you again," he said. He reached an arm across the bed in my direction.

"Well, you did. Here I am." I was an asshole.

"Did you hear the part about how I was scared you'd died? What if you had? What would I do then?"

"I don't want to think about it."

"I didn't say you have to...but listen. Ren, we're in this together, right?"

"In what? Danny, we're not talking, we're not helping each other. I'm stuck here on my own... I can't even go to the store without asking you! I can't go out, I can't get away, I haven't been on my own in ages, and when I do go out you get mad at me because you don't know where I am!" I pulled my belt tight and walked out of the room. Thomas scooted after me. Danny whipped back the covers and followed, too, grabbing a towel from the back of the door to wrap around his waist.

"Renee, what is going on?" Danny grabbed me by the arm. "What are you saying? Do you need more time away? Because we can do that. What do you need?"

"Nothing." I shook him off. In the kitchen, the sun reflected off the painted floorboards, lighting up the cobwebs in the rafters. Thomas crawled into in a sunbeam and sat, chewing on a ball.

"Talk to me, Renee. I was dying last night. I couldn't stand all the things I was imagining about you. I thought you'd been kidnapped or raped or that you'd drowned in the lake, and I couldn't stand it. I went crazy. I got Thomas to sleep and I felt like I was losing my mind. I realized...I realized that I don't want this anymore. I can't stand it."

I stopped. I listened carefully—maybe he would say it. Maybe he wanted change, too.

"Renee, we have to try harder to get along."

I huffed my breath out and looked away.

"What? What did you think I was going to say?"

I continued to stare out the window for a minute longer, then I looked right at him. "I don't want to do this anymore, either."

"Really?" He was excited, ready to reconcile.

"I'm done, Danny. I can't do this. I'm doing a shitty job. I hate it. I..." But he didn't understand me. "I have to go. I can't do it. I have to go and I'm leaving you. And Thomas." I had him by the arms now. He pushed me off, his eyes huge and hurt.

"But you can't just leave."

"Danny, I have to." I was sweating, pleading. My housecoat stuck to my back. My heart beat hard.

"But why, why can't you try some more? Maybe I can fix it." He was leaning in, reaching with his voice to turn me, keep me here.

"You can't fix it! I'm broken! I'm fucking it up! Leaving is the only solution. It's the only way Thomas isn't going to grow up broken, too. I have to leave. Don't try to stop me."

He was quiet, but then, suddenly, like I'd never seen him before, he was angry. His eyes flashed behind his glasses.

His teeth showed under his lip. "You are so selfish! Who the fuck do you think you are that you can call it all off! You don't get to go! You don't get to say, 'I'm done, I quit,' and leave! You're the mother. What am I supposed to do with Thomas! He's not even weaned!"

Thomas began to howl. I scooped him up to shield him from Danny's voice. "He took breast milk in a bottle last night, didn't he? He'll take formula."

"Don't! You're leaving, remember?" He took Thomas from me. He gathered the baby close and hugged him to his chest, rubbing his back and jouncing him. He glared at me, but he seemed calm, and terribly, terribly angry.

I watched them walk toward the window. My sweat cooled. I was already untethered, light-headed, unspooling as they walked away. It was happening and I couldn't process it. Tears welled and spilled down my cheeks.

A second ticked past, and then another. "Where will you go?" he asked.

"Home," I choked out.

He waited a moment, then said to the window: "This is home."

"I meant Vancouver."

He hugged Thomas close, rocking back and forth. "Go now, why don't you. If you're going. Go." He didn't look at me.

"I...I have to gather my things. Get stuff in order."

It was happening too fast. I thought I'd have more time. I'd imagined it differently—the packing, the planning, some sort of soft goodbye.

"Renee," Danny said, turning from the lake, "just go. You made yourself clear. You don't want to be here, so go."

I stared at him, dumb and weeping. My husband. He was different than I thought—same soft face, same smooth skin, but he was tougher, somehow, suddenly real and fierce. I didn't know him, I realized. My son was in his arms, my future; in those two bodies at the window I suddenly saw a future, but I'd already said I was leaving, and Danny was telling me to go. It had stopped being an idea. My knees buckled. I stumbled to the couch.

Thomas batted at dust motes. He talked to his hand. He touched his dad's face. I could smell him. No, I remembered his smell. I shook, remembering the first time I saw his feet. I looked across the distance of the room and thought of the texture of his footed pyjamas, how someone else would wash and fold them—Danny, not me. I'd done this. I tried to breathe.

Danny asked, "Who are you going with?" He swallowed hard. "Did you meet someone at the bar?"

"Yes." I pressed my palms into the pain in my chest. "Glory."

CHORUS
Danny Chance, point at Chance Bay

The first I heard of her was out at Henry's on poker night with all the guys from work.

Halfway through a hand, Paul reached behind him and turned up the volume on a cassette player. The murmuring in the speakers became a woman's voice. I heard bar noises—glasses clinking, chairs scraping the floor, bursts of sudden laughter. Henry stopped shuffling the cards and Bud stopped talking mid-sentence. I took a swig of beer.

Her speaking voice was like broken glass under a car tire, but beautiful, if that makes sense. A single guitar picked out a melody. A banjo joined in. I liked it—the bluegrass sound and the predictable up and down of the song, but then the silk and gravel of her voice sat me back in my chair.

"Who is that?" I asked, as applause rose over the last chords.

Paul laughed that I'd never heard of Glory. He said she wrote the song, that the mountain, the lake, the story of it all happened here. Jacques jumped in and said she was as good as anything on the radio, her and her cousin what's-her-name.

"Crystal," Bud said, chiming in for the first time. Everyone laughed and he flushed.

I kept one ear on the music as Henry dealt and the play went around the table. Glory broke off her songs to chat or drink, but the banjo player, Crystal, was silent despite

Glory's jibes and commentary. Jacques lit another cigarette and Bud won the hand.

I asked Paul how he got the tape. I thought there might be a story in it. One night last year he went drinking at the pub, but he'd forgotten his wallet. She gave him a break, and she got in trouble from the bartender for it, too. He told her he'd make a recording the next time she played, to make it up to her. He'd kept a copy for himself.

Henry started taking the piss out of Paul. "Didn't she say there were other ways of making it up, Paul?"

Paul glared at him. When he'd taken his four track down to the pub, it got him in trouble. Turned out Hardy was in town. The other men nodded and Bud actually winced.

"Who's Hardy?" I'd asked.

Henry squinted through his cigarette smoke and said, "Hardy's a cunt. A wife beater, a child abuser, and what else? A skidder driver, I think. Only in town once in a while. And here's what I don't get." He folded his arms across his chest. "I can see a little fooling around, but I cannot understand a woman who sticks with an asshole like Hardy. I mean, what makes a reasonably intelligent whore demean herself further by hooking up with a guy like that? Unless he pays well, that is."

Paul bit: "She's not a fucking streetwalker!"

Henry winked at us. "She doesn't have to be if everyone knows her phone number."

Bud stood, clapped his hands together, and told us all it was time for a break.

Later, I saw Jacques stretched out in an easy chair in the living room. He had the tape turned up again and the banjo could be heard, tuning, over the noises of the bar. "Side two," he said.

"Who's gonna buy me a beer on my birthday? Huh? Which one of you bastards wants to shell out? I'll make it worth your while..." Glory laughed, but a loud thump and a tape squeal cut her off. "Jesus Christ, Hardy, there's no law says a guy can't buy me a drink. Leave his recording stuff alone! Fucksake. Just forget it. Go sit down, the both of you. Bloody inappropriate, hey, Crystal?" Her voice tapered off and the guitar started.

Crystal's voice joined in, slightly higher, pulling at Glory's so a dissonance wavered between them. The bar noise disappeared and their voices rang in the quiet. Bears and true love, that's what I remember. Blood and death in harmony. When the song ended, I found I'd been holding my breath.

Jacques opened his eyes. "She's a siren, that one."

I misunderstood, thought fire siren, air raids. "What?"

"Calls the sailors in off their boats and drowns 'em."

PART TWO

Where She Goes Between the Songs

CRYSTAL

Glory said, "Be careful what you wish for, sweetheart," and I wanted to slug her. Course we'd had a couple of drinks by then and I'd just finished telling her she could fuck right off. There was this undertow feeling all winter and spring, and I hated how it pulled at us. Everything we did, even if it was good, was strained with this tugging from below—Glory bitching about how we never got any good gigs, how we were stale, how it was better in Vancouver and all we had to do was go. I ignored her. I teased her and changed the subject. I hid the car keys and bought her strings off the Internet so she never had to go into the city and buy them and maybe be tempted by the Greyhound station right near the music store and the one-shot, one-hundred-bucks-to-the-coast, overnight and you wake up at Terminal and Main. No. I pulled just as hard as that undertow to keep us in Fort St. James because here we are famous, and here what we have is good enough: people want to hear us sing, pay us to do so, people keep us in drinks, take us to parties, and drive us home when the fun is over. Who knew what would happen if we went to Vancouver? Where would we live? Who would know about us? We'd have to start all over and we aren't in our twenties anymore. Here we can gather a crowd just by showing up. There we'd be nobodies. And two nobodies can turn into nothing pretty damn fast.

Glory said, "Play, damn you. I can't wait all night."

I lay down my card. "Uno."

"Fuck you," she said, and threw in her hand. We were hardly awake at this point. Even Uno was too much. Glory got us more beers and I tried to relight the candles on the table. I couldn't work the safety on the lighter.

"Here, give it to me."

She took it and lit it in one try. I cracked my beer and took a drink. It didn't taste near as sweet as the first sip I'd had after our set at the pub, but by that point it didn't matter. I'd had about eight more waiting for her to get home, wondering how she'd do it since I took her car. She'd made it eventually, drunker even than I was, and I didn't ask her how. The candles flickered against the plastic sheeting on the windows. We were out on Southside, at Glory's little hideaway. It felt like no one could find us out there, even though everyone knew where it was, but they didn't come if they weren't invited.

"How come you don't have parties out here?"

She lit her smoke. Dragged. Blew out smoke rings. She shrugged. "Don't want to mess it up. Don't want to clean up after. Don't care to share it."

I knew there was more to it. This was her mom's old property. Glory and Anton built the hut after their mom died, and when Glory had that split with her dad and never talked to him again, she started staying out here. It smelled like beeswax and blankets.

We always did our songwriting here. Couldn't do it at my parents' place in town—my brother took that over after Mom and Dad left, and now Richard lived there with his bitchy wife and their friends. No place for me. I was living at the St. James apartments in a room facing the lake. Only had a bed and a fridge and a bathroom, but I didn't need more. I had my banjo. I had Glory's place and Glory. Or I did, up until she started in about leaving.

She lay back on the pillows and the mess of blankets we

had out on the floor. I got down there, too, and found it was much better than trying to stay in my chair at the table. I brought my beer down and pulled the blankets over me. Glory stared at the smoke she exhaled, watching it curl its way up to the rafters and disappear in the shadows. I watched her breathe in and out. I knew every mood, every flaw, every curve and corner of her goddamn mind, and she was planning on leaving. She'd made it plain.

"You think we could rent a place cheap somewhere not on the Downtown Eastside?" She breathed in. "I mean, there's gotta be apartments, or even basements, that don't cost a million bucks. All kinds of people live in Vancouver, like really poor people, so there's gotta be cheaper places." We were stoned, too, so her thoughts meandered. "I bet we could walk to the beach. See the seagulls."

"We got seagulls here. At the dump."

She snorted. "Not dump gulls, ocean gulls. We could watch the boats, Crystal. We could feed the whales."

"What in hell do you feed a whale? Jesus. You want to feed it bread crumbs, like a duck?" I laughed.

"Pop Rocks. I wonder what would happen if you fed a whale Pop Rocks?"

"That's just cruel. Don't you remember what happened when we gave Tiny pop rocks? And he's a human. He cried. A whale would probably inflate or something. Christ, can you imagine?"

It struck us and we were off. We lay there laughing and crying even though it was all leaking under, everything we could count on, draining away because Glory wanted to leave. We laughed until the candles guttered.

I butted out her cigarette when she fell asleep with it still burning in her hand, then I covered her with a blanket. To me, she still looked like my skinned-kneed, dirty-faced little cousin, her black hair all wild on the pillow. She still looked nine to my ten, even if we were old ladies now, thirty-four and thirty-five, still in our hometown, still singing to the same drunks and assholes as we did when we were nineteen and twenty. She slept and all the drinking and the late nights fell away and she was perfect: long lashes resting on her cheeks, the line gone from between her eyebrows, her hands still for once, resting under the weight of all her silver rings.

I sipped my beer and watched her sleep and I knew it was coming to an end, and that hurt. I climbed back into my chair and watched out the window, but I couldn't tell the night from the water through the storm windows. The wind howled. A pine cone fell from a tree and landed on the deck, scaring me, but I stayed at the window, waiting. For what? I didn't know. Something certain to come back. Something as sure as the lake freezing in the winter, the water rising in spring, the way our voices climbed together, no matter where we were or how much we'd had to drink or what would come next, like a tower we were building together, like a lighthouse against the dark. I wanted that.

I wanted something more solid than sand to stand on. We had mattresses on the floor and blankets, but still the cold seeped up from the sand and I knew the beach hut was only here so long as the lake allowed it. Someday a storm would come and wash away the beach to the roots of the cottonwood trees and then those would tumble down, too. Or else the hut would go up in flames. Or we'd be lost out there in the dark, in the deep black lake, like people in one of the songs we wrote.

I blew out the last candle. No fires tonight, at least. I crawled under the blankets next to Glory and set my head down beside hers on the pillow. She woke enough to gather me in and we cuddled up like we had since we were small, sharing a bed, while our parents partied in the next room. I cried a little because the feeling wasn't there like it used to be, when we listened to them laugh and shout next door, that it was us against the world. Now it was just me in the night. Her arms felt good around me, though, and I fell asleep savouring that.

The next morning, I made breakfast on the little two-burner hot plate. I had the bread in the toaster and was stirring the beans while Glory fiddled with her four track and tuned the new strings on her guitar. She hadn't got Tiny and Anton to take off the storm shutters yet, and outside, all blurry and pastel, the sun looked smudged through the layers of no-see-um netting and plastic.

"Tiny still married?" I asked her. It was a joke to get her talking—she always had something to say about her brothers.

"Hmm?" She plucked her E again and tightened the bolt. "Tiny? Yeah. He's with Maureen still. She's pregnant, I think." She sniffed. "Least she acts like it—she's got him running all over the place."

I smiled. "Anton?"

"Nope. Not Anton. My most devoted brother—no loyalty except to siblings, first cousins, dogs, fishing, and drinking."

I laughed because that was Anton for sure; he might have been asexual, for all I ever saw him with a woman. He helped a lot, though, came out just to check on Glory. My brother hung out with us to find out where the party was, but he never looked after me like hers did.

I had this memory of sitting on a dock, four in a line— me and Anton, Tiny and Glory—all of us under ten. Tiny dared Anton to jump off into the water, but it was dark under the dock and there were weeds, and none of us wanted to get in and swim. It must have been out at Cottonwood. I remember all the grown-ups in camp chairs by the fire, laughing and drinking, none of them paying attention. Glory jumped in, I remember. The smallest of us. I saw her hair disappear below the weeds, and then Tiny was in and Anton was in, so I jumped in and none of us could swim very well. None of the grown-ups saw us go in or haul ourselves out onshore, dripping and shaking, scared and covered in snot and tears. We had two towels between us, and Anton and Tiny rubbed us dry and warm. It wasn't nothing. The thought of those weeds and the shadows under the dock still made me shiver.

I broke some eggs into the cast-iron pan. It was getting darker, even though it was morning. It finally, finally felt like spring—storm season was about to start. The wind was up, out of the trees behind us, not off the lake, so we were safe from any real storms. I poked the yolk of one egg with the flipper.

"Glory, remember when you and Anton got the quad stuck up in the bush past Sowchea?"

She snorted.

"I can't believe you guys walked all the way back. What was it—ten K? Twelve?"

"It took us all night to get back. Anton was shitting himself—I don't know any man more scared of bears. I had to sing for hours. Every time I stopped he'd whimper and grab my arm."

I'd heard that story about six hundred times. Sometimes Glory threw in cougars and porcupines to make it more interesting, but it was Anton grabbing her arm I loved. He was the one who used to push us on the swings when we were small. He'd buy us beer, too, if we asked him. He was also the one picked Glory up in Prince George after their mom died and she fucked off to the coast in their mom's old Ford until they put a stop on the credit cards. Anton drove her back here after she hitchhiked up to PG, her belly out to here. Anton never gave her a bad time.

I poked the eggs. "Hey, are you out here for the season?"

She shrugged. "Maybe." She tightened the G. "Hardy's back on Friday."

"That motherfucker."

She shrugged again. Looked at me as if to say, I don't understand it any better than you do.

"Does he come out here?" I looked at the bench where she usually slept, barely wide enough for one. The other benches in the cabin were covered in stuff—sweaters and skirts, underpants, books, tapes. She had skinny bookshelves in between the windows, full of her mom's paperbacks. The windows went from the ceiling down to the benches, and below the benches were shelves with boxes on them. I stood on a wood pallet in front of the eggs. Glory sat at the high plywood bench that stretched the farthest out into the room—her desk, dinner table, candleholder, and, right now, platform for her four track. She usually kept the four track in one of the boxes under the table.

She shook her head. "No. He doesn't like camping out. Gets enough of that in logging camps. Likes to shower. Besides, this is too far from town."

"It's only twenty minutes," I said.

"I know. But that's too long. His trailer's only five minutes from the pub." She set her guitar down and stretched out her back and arms. "Those beans done yet?"

"Almost."

The smell of brown beans wafted up warm and sweet. The wind whapped the plastic against the cabin. We listened for a while in silence.

"What about that other asshole? Todd?" I used as much slime on the name as I could.

She looked away out the window. "What about him?"

"He comes out here, doesn't he?"

She pulled her hair back and started to twist it into a bun. "Yeah. When he's in town."

I knew he came out here. I knew he stayed with her in this little shack and I also knew that if Hardy found out he'd kill them both. Literally. I watched her fuss with her hair out of the side of my eye. She'd been fucking Todd since high school. He was a know-it-all asshole. But gorgeous. One of those good-looking nice guys who can get anything he wants. He went away to school and she was his home fuck; whenever he was in town, they hooked up, and it was awful to watch. Glory was the toughest girl I knew—a rock-hard, nasty piece of work, sometimes, but with him? Forget it. She was just a hopeless girl. And not his only girl, either. He had girlfriends in Vancouver. He had enough money to fly Glory out there anytime, but he didn't. He came back in his good leather shoes and fancy jackets and he charmed her. They were a public secret—thought no one knew about them, but we all knew.

Hardy was hardly even civil with other humans, and there were rumours about him I didn't want to believe— that he had a family back in Ontario he'd either killed or assaulted or abandoned, or he broke out of a maximum-security prison and got away. He treated Glory rougher than shit and he scared me, but somewhere in their fucked-up relationship there was enough mutual meanness to make them equal. Todd had a different hold on her. He froze her, somehow. She was still that high-school girl for him, but he was all grown-up—a lawyer in the city. He made her small and she waited for him and I hated to see it.

"Is he coming back soon?"

She kept looking out the smeary window. "Don't know."

In a way, I could see how she was stuck—Hardy was a source of money, sex, and some prestige because he would beat the shit out of anyone who sneezed in his direction. A girl might benefit from associating with that. But Todd confused me—she seemed to get nothing out of his homecoming but a whole lot of fear that Hardy would find out. She was wasting herself on him. There was no way in hell he would ever take up with her permanently, so he wasn't a plane ticket out of here and he wasn't a meal ticket while he was here—in fact, he sponged off her the whole time he was home.

Well, I sort of got it. He had this way he'd drop his chin and look at you with his brown eyes like you were the only important thing on earth. He could melt anyone. Glory told me he just had to bat his lashes to get promoted. He got good marks in school, good jobs out of school, and now he was in the news for doing work for some Coastal Native Band on land-rights issues. Or something. If I heard his name on the radio, I changed the channel.

I licked the spoon. "Todd ever say anything about coming here permanent?" I was pushing my luck talking about it.

She looked at me slow and cool, careful to show nothing, which hurt more than a sharp answer because as if I didn't know how broke up about it she was. "What do you think?"

My turn to shrug. I'd heard her cry about him before and I'd hear it again.

"He might come up for midsummer. Anyway. What about you?" she asked.

"What about me?"

"You shacking up with anybody these days?"

I rolled my eyes. "I'm making you breakfast, what does that say?"

"Nothing." She grinned. "You're only domestic for me."

She made me sound so stupid.

I said, "I been thinking about Bud."

"Bud Shinnerd? Christ, Crystal."

"Shut up."

"Okay, okay, but Bud? Wasn't that in high school?"

Oh, high school. If I let myself go there, I could almost feel the flannel of his new-hay-and-deodorant-smelling shirts, or see the golden fuzz on his neck. I wanted him looking at me, all gangly and sixteen again. But he was a man, now, with ginger sideburns and workboots, and I had no way to go back in time and fix it all. It made my throat ache. "Yeah. So? I was only thinking about him. I heard he's been hanging out with that rich guy down the bay. The one up from Vanderhoof, bought that doctor's house."

"Henry. Yeah, I heard that, too, the big log place on the lake. But why are you thinking about Bud? You don't wanna drag all that stuff out again, do you?"

I kept my back to her.

"Well, whatever. You do what you want. I'll be out here if you need me."

She'd been out here all winter, but I didn't mention it. She had no phone and I had no idea when I was welcome. Some partnership. We'd hardly written at all since the fall. I didn't say that, though. I sniffed.

Glory leaned over and rewound the tape in the four track. "Listen to this," she said, and pressed Play.

I expected familiar first chords but they weren't. These notes were new—slow and sure where Glory usually strummed loose and rough. Two run-throughs of a sad-sounding opening four bars and then her voice. I liked it. The toast popped up, and I started to butter it while I listened. The words were harsh but clear and her voice played no tricks. I listened for the space behind and above them where my voice would go, and for the hollow between her notes where the banjo would fit, but instead I heard the second track she'd laid down on the first—her own guitar in counterpoint, and then her voice harmonizing with her melody.

I looked at her but she was watching the wind bend the willows out the plastic windows. The song lurched up higher and higher, the chorus bitching and begging at the same time, home, and drown and run, the lyrics crying. I smelled the beans burning. I stirred them and heard the end of the first song of Glory's she'd written with no part in it for me.

"What do you think?" she asked.

I said nothing.

When we were girls there was no place I imagined going that didn't include her, especially in music. I hitched my banjo to her guitar and sang under and around her like scaffolding, and here she was writing songs without me in them. What could I say? I turned off the heat under the eggs.

"Get a plate," I said. "It's ready." I poured two half glasses of vodka and cracked the seal on a bottle of orange juice. "Don't you have any fucking ice?"

CHORUS

*Tim Johnny, list written on foolscap tucked
in the back of his high-school yearbook*

Times I fell for Glory Stuart:

• Grade 2 when she wore a pink shirt, pink skirt, pink socks, pink barrettes, pink leg warmers, pink panties, and she charged twenty-five cents for us to see them.

• The time she kissed me on a dare in Grade 10 science when Mr. Holmes was out of the room. She kissed Ross Winston, too, but she kissed me longer.

• At Lou-Ellen Parker's wedding, when she was drunk and spent an hour holding my hand and saying how much she loved her cousin Crystal.

• When she sang "Knockin' on Heaven's Door" at Pat's funeral.

• When she sang that Pixies song at Dean's funeral.

• When she stayed hugging Dean's bawling wife for so long after everyone else left because they didn't know what to do.

• The time she sang that song about coming up Highway 27 home right after I come back from the oil patch. And every other time she sang it.

- Whenever she brought me a can of Pacific Pilsner without me asking for it when she was serving at the pub.

- The time I drove her home and she puked on the wheel of my truck and she told me I was her hero because I didn't deck her for it.

- The time she sang Pink Floyd at the end of the midsummer festival before they lit the bandstand on fire. How she kept singing it all night. How happy she was to see the sunrise later, and how we were still hanging out. How all that night she made me hide her from Hardy because he saw her kiss that asshole Brent Redder when she finished her set, then he beat the shit outta Brent and the ambulance came. When I hid her in my tent and she told me about her brothers and the crazy shit they did when they were all kids.

- When she thanked me by giving me a hand job.

- When next time I saw her sing at the pub, she winked at me like, Oh yeah, I know you.

- When she sang her song about growing up on the river, about being a little girl in the tall grass.

- When she'd put her hand on my shoulder when I left her big tips at the pub when she was pregnant.

- When her face got all cute and chubby when she was pregnant.

- When she got crazy after the baby came and everybody hated her and she shot a hole in the school with her brother's gun and she told me I was the only one who came to see her in the drunk tank.

- When she sang "Last Night in Middle River" not even strumming her guitar, the time Crystal was in the hospital with mono. That was the year the old folks' home burned down. Maybe it was the fundraiser for that she was singing at. Man, that song.

- Yesterday, when I seen her at the liquor store in that short skirt and bra.

CRYSTAL

I hitchhiked into town. Caught a ride with my former high-school principal, which wasn't exactly comfortable, but it got me to the reserve. I'd walk to town from there. I answered all his questions about my life with shrugs and maybes and steered him onto the topic of Glory—everyone would rather talk about her, anyway. It got me off the hook. My mind was on her, anyway, the fight that busted out over our beans on toast, the curses I'd chucked at her. I had her stupid new song stuck in my head.

We'd been into our second drink, the second time around the argument tree, her calling me names, me going silent, freezing her out, when someone knocked at the door. She jumped up and opened it and it was the woman from the parking lot. The pretty one with the short hair and the baby. This time, she had no baby. Only a story about being kicked out, about Glory inviting her to run away, and then Glory did invite her. She invited her to stay in the little hut on the bay that she'd said was so sacred. I really gave it to Glory then. I screamed myself hoarse. I threw the four track. I made the woman cower in a corner while Glory laughed. I hit her in the mouth for that and then left. Glory got in a couple of good shots, too, but I could still feel her mouth on my knuckle, the way her lip gave and shifted over her teeth.

She'd been determined to leave before, but she said she actually had something lined up in Vancouver this time. She spat that at my back as I was leaving, said she'd do better without me. I tried to shuck it off as I walked. I needed a way out of my head, or some way to get her out of my head.

This kid walking through the crossroads at Four Corners was just the distraction I was looking for. New boots, new backpack, new jacket. Fuck it, I thought.

"Hey," I shouted. "Are you a tree planter?"

He stopped in the median, his boots on top of flowers I'd seen a road crew putting in the ground yesterday. "What?!" he shouted back, looking around to see if I meant him. He pulled his earbuds out, hung them around his neck, and started across the road. He slowed before he reached me, so I put myself to work, stretching around to reach Glory's smokes, which I'd stuck in my purse before I left, just to piss her off, so my shirt would ride up and show off my back.

"Hey," he said, pretty quiet-like.

"Hey," I said, playing it cool. "Wanna smoke?"

"I don't smoke," he said, shaking his head and looking away.

"So, are you tree planting? You with Zodiac's crew?"

"No." He looked a little impatient. "I'm just looking for work. I heard you can get on at the mill pretty easy. They pay good."

I looked at him and measured that. "Nah. They're not hiring. Rumours of a shutdown." I watched his face fall. Then I took pity on him. "There're other things to do here." I fumbled the cigarette and dropped it on the ground like a dork and had to pretend I didn't care. "There's always someone going into the bush or out of the bush. They're surveying out at the Nation River, even. They might be looking for someone." I didn't know what I was talking about. Glory told me she served supper to some surveyors last week at the pub and they'd said they were out at the Nation. I moved in to nudge his arm. "Don't worry about it. Stick with me and we'll find you something."

He looked doubtful, but walked with me. "So, what do you do here for fun?"

"Oh, we have fun." I smiled a little wickedly. "We have lots of fun, sometimes. You been down to the lake yet?"

"Yeah." He smiled. "It's big. Way bigger than I thought it'd be."

I watched him as we walked. I liked his tidy hair and sloppy jeans.

"I mean, I looked at a map, but I didn't think it would take up so much of the landscape."

"It's big alright. Big and cold. It's not much use for swimming." He was actually listening, so I tried to make it better. "But the fishing's good. They say."

"You don't fish?"

"Nah. My cousins do, but I do other things." He looked at me like he expected me to elaborate. "So, what's your name?" I asked, thinking now's about the time to change the subject.

"Boyd. You?"

"Crystal." We walked down Main to where it started to curve. I needed to make this guy see something good about me. He was pretty indifferent, but I'd get him. "You wanna see what we do for fun around here? Follow me."

Eleven o'clock on a spring morning's not the best time to be looking for fun in Fort St. James, but I knew the day shift at the Cabaret, and though they wouldn't open until noon, I figured Polly would let me in early. I banged on the loading door.

"Polly!" I yelled, and grinned at Boyd. He was looking doubtfully around at the empties and the wrinkled old condoms spread like dead worms on the asphalt. Behind the Cab, there's sometimes a party after hours, but it usually dies down when someone falls off the drop, where the pavement breaks off into what would be a jetty if it were over water, but since it's over a cliff that ends in broken bottles and lakeshore, it's just a party hazard. Boyd walked over and looked off the edge. Polly opened the door.

"What do you want, Crystal?" She looked like she'd been dragged behind a cart; her hair was stringy and sticking out all over and her eyes were deeply bagged, last night's makeup still on her lids.

"Jesus, Polly, you alright?"

"Yeah, just too early to start work. I think I'm still drunk." We both laughed. "Who's yer friend?" She jerked her head at Boyd. "He's pretty cute."

"This is Boyd. Thought I'd bring him by to see if we could get coffee. What do you say?"

Polly looked behind her into the gloom of the entry dock toward the kitchen. "I guess it's alright. It's just me here and Roy, and Roy's sleeping in the storeroom. Just keep it quiet, okay?"

"Sure, sweetie, no problem." I smiled at Boyd and squeezed in the door. Polly left little room, so Boyd had to squeeze past her, too.

"You travelling, little man?" she asked, leaning in close.

"He's deciding," I told her, and boldly took his hand. He was so surprised, he let me.

Inside the Cabaret, the smell of beer was dampened by the breeze off the lake. Polly had all the windows open on the lake side of the building, and where the sun made it through the fuggy glass, dust motes scrambled up and down the shafts of sunlight. Boyd and I sat at a table near a window. He looked around with high eyebrows. He whistled.

"Man, I've been in some dives, but this…"

"What's wrong with this?" I stood to get us coffee from the pot brewing behind the bar.

"This is probably the worst-looking bar I've ever seen."

"Not a bar. A cabaret." I poured an ample shot of Bailey's in the bottom of the mugs.

"Seriously, this is a weird place." He squinted at the vinyl booths and the worn, diamond-patterned carpeting.

"That's just because you can see it. At night when you're at a bar, the lights are off and there are too many people to get a good look at a place." He shook his head in disbelief. I was surprised by how defensive I felt. "I bet the bars in the city aren't so fancy. Drink your coffee."

I set the mugs on the table and sat down in a sunbeam. The vinyl was hot under my thighs. I could feel the heat seeping into my jeans. Boyd drank a mouthful and his eyebrows shot up again. I laughed.

"I spiked it. You don't mind, do you?"

He relaxed then, and leaned back in the booth. That's good, I thought. The more relaxed, the better. If he was relaxed, then I could relax. It wasn't usually me who got the boys; I'm too awkward and cautious. Boys were Glory's specialty. She just had to smile a certain way and she could have any man from here to Tache. I'm the quiet one. I let her lead and that usually got me what I wanted, but if she was leaving I was going to have to learn to take care of myself. What would it be like if she actually left? Didn't bear thinking about. I focused on Boyd. "Funny name, Boyd."

"Not really. It's my mother's grandfather's last name. Irish, I think. Or English."

I grinned. "Do people call you 'Boy'?"

"No. Generally, they call me Boyd. But sometimes they call me 'Sir'."

I laughed because he wanted me to.

"They call me Sweetcheeks McGee. Cheers."

We clinked glasses. He told me about his new boots. I told him about the bar. He told me about the bus ride here, and I listened closely because someday I might make that same trip to find Glory, if she managed to leave.

I brought a bottle of rum over to the table. I snuck it a bit, inside my jacket, so Polly wouldn't see, but she was clanking around in the washrooms. She'd be opening up soon, and I figured we'd blend right in, then, with the other afternoon drinkers. I poured a liberal measure into our mugs once the coffee was gone, and we clinked glasses again.

"Boyd, I gotta tell you, this is not my usual thing." He looked at me, confused. "It is a weird and serious event for me to get drunk with a stranger in the middle of the day and we are well into it, but I want you to know, we'll go there together, okay?"

Still confused but entertained, he nodded. "Sure, Sweetcheeks, you got it. I thought you did this every day. You're not telling me you're a lightweight, are you?"

I blushed.

Polly brought some fries over once they opened the grill. "You guys," she said, and shook her head. We were glassy-eyed and open-mouthed, laughing at ourselves. "You be careful!" We ate the fries and ordered more.

I saw Anton and Tiny come in off the street a while later. I stood and waved at them. "Boyd, this is Tiny. Don't listen to him, 'cause he's got bad ideas. And this is Anton. Don't piss him off. Seriously. The last guy pissed him off was buried last weekend." Anton grinned. Boyd held out his hand.

"What're you and Glory doin' later, Crystal?" Tiny pulled up a chair and dug his fingers into the fries. "You goin' to the party?"

Anton held up two fingers for Polly. They had full glasses with them already. He grabbed a chair and sat at the end of our booth.

"I dunno." I raised my eyebrows at Boyd. It was a question. I felt close to him; we had the tie that holds strangers together when they've been drinking from the same bottle. I felt warm all over. If I were Glory I'd make my move now—

scoot out from my side of the booth and over into his. "You feel like going to a party?"

"What kind of party?"

She would move his red coat out of her way and slide closer. He'd go for it, too—put his arm around her, pull her close. But I wasn't Glory. I sipped my drink.

"Bush party," Anton said. "We're not going. We're going fishing." He glared at Tiny, making some kind of point.

"Lake's too rough for fishing," Tiny said. "Let's just go to the party."

"It's gonna rain. I'd rather fish than get rained on at some pit party in the bush."

"It'll rain on the lake, too." Tiny rolled his eyes at his brother, making me laugh.

Around us, things were picking up momentum: the Tragically Hip jammed out of the jukebox, and every seat at the bar was taken by men in jeans and workboots. Polly swatted a customer with a bar rag. He leaned back, mock-affronted, and roars of laughter poured out from all the mouths down the bar. The sunlight had changed in our time indoors—a low afternoon glare shone up, highlighting the bags under Boyd's eyes as he tried to find a wireless signal on his phone. He'd never find one. The heat in the bar made me sleepy. I let my eyes slide around at the mid-afternoon clientele. I loved the jerks, mostly, and I loved hating the ones I didn't love. Sue-Ann from the Shell station was there with her man, a big guy who worked for the town road crew. I could see Anton eyeing him up. Lola and Shayanne were doing pull-tabs, a big pile of not-a-winners growing between their glasses. Some bush crew was in and the old guys sat in a bunch at the back. No one sat near the dance floor yet, but that would start up soon enough. It was Saturday, after all.

Everything else would start up, too—the spats from the gossip going around the bar, the snubs and the fights.

Old, invisible hurts and hardships would seep out like water on ice. Sly glances would turn into glares. Someone would make a pass at someone else's wife, and insults, then fists, would fly. Suddenly, I felt too hot, pissed off about this place and these people. Boyd looked stupid in his stiff new clothes and boots. Anton and Tiny were morons, just like the rest of them. I looked around and all I could see were missing teeth and mean, squinty eyes. I was sorry I'd brought Boyd here. I wished instead we'd kept walking out toward the point, through downtown, and out the other side, so he'd see some good. Some other thing than this beer-soaked mess. Glory would leave me here to shrivel and die with these losers. I caught Boyd staring at my tits. I realized I deserved it. I'd led him on like Glory would've. I'd been Glorying it up all day. Since when did I pick up strangers in the road and get them drunk? I stood up.

"Going to the bathroom." I lurched away.

Once I'd pissed, avoiding my eyes in the bathroom mirror, I kept going out the front door and back onto the street. It was later than I'd thought, coming on evening, and the wind was up. The cool air soothed my hot cheeks. I walked down the hill into town. The stores were closing, the ones that weren't boarded up, and the trucks running outside the Overwaitea left plumes of exhaust in the air. I followed the road toward the lake. Boyd could find himself a new guide. I'd lost my hard-on. I wanted only wind.

A band of clouds rested on the horizon, so the sun hung hidden as it set. The clouds were rimmed with gold. I loved that sky so much it hurt. It felt like no one in this town ever looked up. I thought of the hundreds of blurred sunsets Glory and I had sung through at the beach hut. I walked by the bandstand in Cottonwood Park and sat down on the edge of the stage. The view when we played here was water, mountain, sky, water. Miles of it. Worlds of it.

What if we never sang together again? What if the last time had already happened? When we sang, when we were inside the song, there was no Glory and no me. There was no audience, no waiting for Christmas or summer or some new thing to come down the pipe, just our fingers and our voices. Sometimes it felt like we were barking or wailing, and that's just what we had to do—I had to pull at Glory's voice, tear it down, replace it with mine, and then sometimes she would climb back up, and for a second our two voices would share the same wave, stretching and slipping back. Then the steel of the strings, a break, and then we came crashing down.

When we were girls, we sang at family barbecues and birthday parties. We were cute, at the start—funny and awkward, with messy hair and corduroy hand-me-down pants from our brothers. I remember aunties pinching our cheeks. Glory was always the leader. She had a big voice, even then, and I'd do whatever she told me. Uncle Dave bought us guitars when we were ten. Glory got really good at hers, but mine didn't make the sounds I wanted it to. Later, when I saw a bluegrass band at the summer festival, I knew I wanted a banjo, just didn't know how to get it. Glory said we'd make money singing and I believed her, so we sang everywhere we could—at parties, grad, outside the liquor store—a cousin novelty act with no competition. We made some cash. I traded in my Yamaha for a second-hand banjo and I learned to pick. First time I got a clawhammer going, we screamed in joy.

Glory's always been a hog and a crowd-stealer, with that smile and that hair. I never stood a chance. But alone, she was half an act and she knew it. She needed me to fill out the sound, back her up, make her realer than real. She'd never admit it, but she owed me a lot. Maybe it was her who helped me come up with banjo money, but it's me who helped her get gigs, it's me who held her voice up when it wanted to fall. It's me who held back her hair when she was gagging over the toilet.

I never loved anyone as hard as I loved her. I've never hated someone so hard, neither. You can't tell me there's nothing in that. If I never did anything better than that, I'd still have done better than most. There was nothing else I wanted, just us. The songs. Glory's voice raising mine as close as it was ever going to get to heaven. Mine raising hers higher than it ever would've got on its own.

I felt so sick, so lonely and small and cheated. Then I got mad. Who did she think she was? She couldn't leave me behind. I was the one who thought up the melodies, even if everyone liked the words better—she'd have nowhere to put the words if she didn't have a melody.

I sat on the edge of the bandstand and fumed. Who would I be, if I wasn't half of her? Maybe no one. I stood up quick, making my head reel. Me and Glory were on the verge of something so big I couldn't get my mind around its edges.

This was worse than when her baby was born. When she kicked me out of the hospital, her all weak and sick on the bed with the baby wrapped up tight in a yellow blanket in the bassinet beside her. I'd walked down the street to Hardy's house. I didn't know what I was going to do, but I'd seen Glory through a screaming hell and I wanted him to know it. I should have known better—I didn't even know if the baby was his. When he hit me with the flat of his hand and knocked the wind out of me, it was that I was thinking of—maybe it wasn't his kid. I didn't go back to the hospital after that. I didn't want Glory to see my split lip and the bruise around my eye. But I didn't need to go. She sorted it out without me. I'd had this secret vision of Glory and me raising the girl out at Southside, making money I don't know how, buying formula, singing songs. Glory gave the baby away to her dad and went on a legendary bender. Uncle Mac having the baby turned out alright, but there was part of me felt cheated out of that, too: a little baby that could have been half-mine and a future where Glory needed me to keep her and our little family afloat.

I hitchhiked out to the coast after Juniper was born, after I found out Glory'd given her away. Through the windows of strangers' cars, I saw the Skeena surge out toward the Pacific Ocean, seals pop up in the salty river water near Port Edward, then Rupert. It was only natural to keep going once I got there. I caught the ferry to the Charlottes and holed up in a hostel for a few nights until I found my feet.

That was the longest we were ever apart, that summer after Juniper was born. Ten years ago, now. I met a logger in Queen Charlotte City who bought me coffee, then supper, then gave me a place to stay for a month. It was easy enough to leave. I never met his wife. I didn't have to deal with the aftermath of a ghost lover on an island the size of a nickel.

The wind was getting serious and I was drunk and sad with it, even as the heat from the drink wore off. I shivered. I started walking again. I took the scenic route around the bay to the foot of the mountain. I wasn't thinking about it, but I knew where I was going: Mac and Juniper's. I wanted to be in a home, a homemade home, so I could quit feeling like I was sick or broken. They would take me in, like they always did, and give me tea and cake. Juniper was a little baker. That made me smile. Her mother sure as hell wasn't.

The road climbed, once past the wooden church, over a hill, the marina down below. I walked fast to get warm. No cars passed. The lake was rippled with the first little stirrings of waves.

What got me most about Juniper was her looks: she looked like a china teacup, that breakable and that beautiful. You could see through her skin to her veins. She cut her hair short this winter and she looked like Beaker from the Muppets, but also like a pixie. Mac loved her. He didn't talk much, but he loved her and she knew it. He was a good grandpa-dad.

I'd watched him fade and turn dumb when Glory's mom died. All that spring, when he and Glory sat at her bedside and watched the cancer eat her, I saw what it did to them—June, who'd always been nut-brown from the sun, faded from spending so much time in bed, then Glory turned hard and mean, and Mac, old Mac who used to take us for walks and tell us legends about the soapalally and the bear brothers, lost his will to speak because nothing he could say would save her. She died and their family exploded.

Anton and Tiny, who were already halfway gone, disappeared into the bush or the bar. Mac went back home to their place on Chance Bay and shut the gate, shut the blinds, holed up, determined never to come out. Glory just left. She didn't say much when she got back and she didn't have to tell me she didn't want to be back. I could see it in her. The skin was tight across her face and she looked like she'd shrunk even though her belly was huge. She was funny about the pregnancy to begin with, but after June died, she didn't even once touch her belly that I saw. Then, she did what the town will never forgive her for, and what broke my heart—instead of the fairy-tale songs-and-roses-falling-in-love-with-the-baby redemption everyone expected, Glory gave the baby away. To her dad, sure, but she still gave her away. Even the softest of the hard-assed won't forgive her for that.

What they don't know is that Mac roused to raise that girl and built the both of them a decent life. That kid knows every bush and berry in these woods for miles around. Word around town is Mac quit talking completely, but I've heard a word or two come out of his mouth, all kind, except if the topic is Glory. Juniper's perfect and it's because she's got Mac, and what no one cares to understand is she's got Mac because of Glory. Simple as that.

I went to their place whenever I was tired or when I needed proof that the world wasn't so bad. I used to read to Juniper sometimes, but mostly I just slept on their couch. It was the one place in town I could be sure I wouldn't run into Glory—it was another little hideaway. So, of course I headed there now.

Thing is, it's three miles from town. I walked on the muddy shoulder, but it was slippery and I was drunk, so I walked in the road. There wasn't any traffic. Until Bud Shinnerd showed up.

He roared up beside me in his F-150, grinning and shouting over the noise. He killed the engine. "Hey there, Crystal. It's been a long time since I seen you."

"Fuck you, Bud."

"Hey!"

I started walking again. I heard him open his truck door and jump out.

"Crystal! Wait up."

He knew enough not to touch me. He matched my stride and walked with me, not talking, and it was good that he didn't talk, because sparks were flying off me, I was so hot. Bud Shinnerd! I glanced back and saw his truck door opened wide to the road.

"You left your truck door open. It's gonna get ripped off."

"Someone will shut it for me." The ever-optimist.

"First they'll steal your stereo, then they'll shut your door."

He shrugged. "Don't matter. The keys are in the ignition. If they want it, they can have it."

I stopped. "Dammit, Bud, that's just stupid. You go shut that door so nobody steals your shit."

He smiled. "Nothing good in there, anyway, except one

CD and it's pretty old. I was hoping maybe you'd give me a new one."

Now, that pissed me off. He didn't know our music was a sore spot, but it smarted to get hit there all the same. "If all's you got is shit, all's you got is shit, don't even pretend that old CD of ours is any good."

"I'm not pretending, Crystal." He peeked at me from under his giant eyebrows. "I never was."

He stared at me till I wanted to slap the eyes out of his head.

I ran away from him up the road toward the lookout. I knew he would follow.

At the lookout, there's a monument to the old Hudson's Bay Fort, a model of a boat with sails, a plaque and a little fence around it. By the time Bud caught up with me, I'd knocked off the mast with a log I found and was winding up to take the nose off the boat, too.

"Jesus, Crystal! Stop it."

"Why?" I swung and the nose of the boat went sailing off the point. "Why should I? This place never did me any favours." I wound up again.

"What's wrong? Why're you so mad?"

I kicked a chunk of plaster, the log over my shoulder like a baseball bat. "I never once got a break. I never once had an easy time of it. Glory's bloody leaving and I'm stuck here in this shithole to do what? What can I do?"

"Glory's leaving?"

"I just said so, didn't I?"

"But what about your band?"

I gave him a glare.

"What did she say?"

"Nothing." I smashed my log down on the boat's middle, and it stuck in the hollow innards. I tugged, but it wouldn't come out. I screamed at it, embarrassed and furious that

Bud was seeing me act like a lunatic.

He came over and pulled the log out for me. I took it and swung again, sending the rest of the mast off the point. I wound up and smashed the boat's hull, but the log stuck again and I fell over it, landing on my ass. Bud smothered a laugh. I jumped up and decked the fucker in the eye. He didn't see that coming, but he did see the next one I lined up. He caught my fist and grabbed me around the waist and sat me in his lap. I struggled, I really meant to punch him again, but he had me tight. I melted in his lap and started to cry.

"Crystal. Don't cry. Shhhh," he said to me. He held me and talked nonsense and I sobbed and listened to his voice and it felt so good. His breath against my ear, my tears wetting the front of his shirt. I could have been sixteen again.

Us at sixteen had just as much fists and hysterics, all mine, and just as much shrugging and grinning, all his. We only went out for two seasons, one winter and spring, and I'd never been so happy and crazy at the same time. It was so messy—I was all over the shop.

The only good memory I kept from that time was a day in February. We'd walked out from town onto the lake ice, just talking and walking. We followed Ski-Doo tracks out toward the horizon, then stopped, and I don't know how long we stayed there, but the sky wheeled around us like the earth was still for once and no time passed. I stared at his face for what could've been hours. I told him every single thing I was going to do in my life and he listened. And after that I couldn't help but break up with him, because I didn't end up doing even one of those things. The planet turned and time passed and all we got was older. Every time I seen him in town since then he's smiled at me like it's okay with him, he understands. There's almost nothing worse than him smiling at me. Except if he didn't.

I cried and cried and he sat us down under the Saskatoon bushes and held me. Night came for real and the bats started up zipping through the bushes. Bud watched them and I leaned on his chest and listened to him breathing.

There are so many parts of me I'd get an eraser and rub out if I could. I'd wipe out how bad I'd been to Bud. I'd wipe out the parts where me and my brothers used to hide under the bed when Dad got rough with Mom; how I stole nail polish and lipstick with Glory; how I've been so jealous of her ever since we were four and I figured out we were two people, not one. I'd spent so much time wishing I was different than I was, and hating the world, cause I wasn't, that I was exhausted. I could've slept on Bud's chest, but I didn't. I listened to his heartbeat and the lake against the shore and my eyes dried and we stayed tangled quietly together.

I'd told Glory that morning she could fuck off and leave if she was going to, it wouldn't hurt me none, but it hurt so much. Glory leaving was like someone ripping out the carpet after each step I took. And that other woman standing there, listening to all of it. Who was she that Glory'd invite her in, make plans with her instead of me?

Bud's chest was better than anyplace I could imagine, and now that I was there, I couldn't bear to leave it. He stroked my hair and didn't speak. It felt like, on the bluff above the old road with the lake in front of us and the mountain behind us, we'd built a little shelter out of nothing but our bodies. It was so simple. It was enough. I might have slept a little, sitting there. I might have slept forever if he hadn't wakened me.

"Crystal? You asleep?"

"No. Course not." I rubbed my eyes.

"You still drunk?"

I laughed.

"You still mad?"

I said nothing.

"Where d'you wanna go now?"

"Mac's."

"You want me to take you there?"

Only thing I could do was nod.

We stood up and brushed off the leaves and dirt. Bud checked out the monument.

"Jeez, Crystal, you did a number on that boat."

I turned my back on it and continued to brush myself down.

"You know why it's a boat, don't you?" I knew he'd tell me. "The fur traders used to sail up the lake to Babine Portage once the water was open. When the schooner made it back to the fort, it was the first time the men had seen flour and tobacco since before freeze-up. They partied like crazy when the schooner came in. D'you know they used to eat the dogs if they got too hungry in winter? One time they wrote that in the factor's journal at New Year's: *Ate the dogs*."

I looked at him to see if he was making it up. "How do you know that stuff?"

He blushed, picked up a chunk of boat, and threw it off the point. "I read in the archives sometimes."

I was surprised. I didn't know he read.

"It's free," he said. "They let anyone in there. And it's really good. They'll copy big sections out of the factor's journals if you want them." He came close to pick a leaf out of my hair. "I made friends with the caretaker last winter when I helped him cut up a tree that'd come down on the fence. He told me some stories. I got hooked."

His hand stayed in my hair. In high school, my hair was always long, longer even than Glory's but straighter, and I remembered Bud gathering it up off my neck once and holding it in a thick rope.

He touched my face all over with his eyes and then he leaned in to kiss me. I stopped him just as his moustache tickled my lip.

"Tell me more about the boat," I said.

He took my hand and I let him, and we walked back down to his truck.

CHORUS
Duane Fairman, the Cabaret

That song cracked open like an egg, like a piece of wood splintered off a chunk and went wailing through the air. It smacked like a frozen snowball on a concrete wall, and you know what? It fuckin' floored me, even though I'd heard her sing every Friday night since forever. But if you ask me, and no one asks, I'd say she's close to done. She looks pissed off and closed up and she don't cry after a good song anymore—she's through breakin' wide open so everyone can see in.

She's just tryin' to get a buck or two whorin' the songs, but I can see she wants outta here. Did anyone ever ask her what she wants? Not fuckin' likely. She's bound by the tonsils to the notes in her guitar—one strum and she's busted up and wailing. This town owns her and she knows it. They tell her every goddamn chance they get, but who in hell else would carry them like she does? She's their stairway up. Fuck. She's like those fingers of God you get, way out on the lake, after weather, when the clouds slit open a bit and the sun shines through and spikes down to the water and you know even though it's been shitty here on earth, up in the sky it's all larks and breezes. Yeah, she's the fuckin' fingers of God.

I'm leavin', too, first chance I get. I'm sick of drunks and hangovers, assholes and songs and girls that break my heart. I know she's sick of it, too. What the hell is here for her? What? That secret kid of hers? Memories? She's got songs. Nothin' else. I've got nothin' 'cept her songs. 'Cept thoughts. 'Cept maybe the storms that tear down the lake every spring. Maybe someday they'll rip the front off the church, steal the stained glass, and smash it on the beach. That would be something.

I only remember heartbreak and sorrow, like a fuckin' country song. My heart gets tore up like my hands when I fall down drunk on a gravel road. Every fuckin' day there's something pullin' at me every which way I turn—some memory, some ghost. I'm sick of ghosts! I want no past. No old selves waitin' to be remembered at every street corner. I want the future and, goddamn, I want it now. Tonight! And I don't care who knows it. I'm done. But her? She's not done yet. She's got a town full of sinners to sing up to heaven. She's tethered to the earth by them. Them and her cousin and her lead-heavy heart. That's all. And yes, you can buy me another.

CRYSTAL

Mac had the fire going when we drove up, burning brush from the lane and winter blowdown from the big firs that hemmed his place in. We could see his silhouette against the flames.

Bud cleared his throat. "Been a long time since I talked with Mac Stuart, Crystal."

"Just don't expect him to talk back."

"He don't go into town much anymore, hey? I can't remember the last time I seen him. Or the girl. What's her name?"

"Juniper. All's you need to know is that she's ten, so that means it's ten years since Auntie June died and ten years since Mac retired and holed up out here. And everything's great out here." I shot him a look. "No matter what you heard."

He patted my leg and opened his door. The sound of the lake poured in: waves racketing the beach, rocks rolling, water smashing onto the point. I stepped out of the truck and into the wind. Bud and I walked together toward the fire.

"Hey, Uncle Mac," I said, stopping a good few feet from him. Bud followed my lead.

"Mr. Stuart," he said.

Mac smiled and saluted us. I knew right away he was happy to see me with Bud.

The screen door slammed and Juniper ran out of the cabin. She tackled me and I staggered into the bush, laughing. Nothing on earth feels so good as that kid's arms around my neck.

"Where've you been! It's been like fifty years since you were here! I wanted to show you my stuff! Who's this? Why's your face all puffy?" She held my face in her hands and moved it into the firelight so she could see it.

I squeezed her, then pushed her off. "This is Bud. He gave me a ride out here."

"Why's he got a black eye?"

Mac shot me a look. Bud smiled and tipped his ball cap at Juniper, then he started hauling brush to the fire with Mac.

Juniper rattled on non-stop, filling me in on school and her baking, how she'd almost burned the cabin down but cleverly thought to use the fire extinguisher. She told me about the ice coming off, how the cabin down the bay had people in it again, how the old folks next door told her she was almost big enough to drive their boat on her own. I thought about her out here all the time with all the old folks; Chance Bay wasn't exactly a hot spot for kids, but I knew, too, that she'd get no more loving place in her life here, with Mac and the Swannells next door and the old doctor and his wife at the other end of the bay. I wondered who it was in the Chance cabin. We sat on the stoop while the men worked. She talked and Mac and Bud bent and hurled, the fire almost smothering with each load until the flame took and swelled and sparked up behind them as they bent to their next load. The fire lit the huge Doug fir trunks and coloured them orange, making their ridges look deep and rough; it filled the clearing between Mac's cabin and his shop, and the woods all around felt nicer because of the heat. It didn't press in like sometimes the dark could when you sat at a campfire. I listened to Juniper and wondered if this feeling was just what I got here, at their place, or if it was the booze finally wearing off. I just felt full up, and it was a familiar feeling, like I'd been waiting for it a long time.

After a while, Juniper went in to put the kettle on. Mac caught Bud's attention and they both came to sit with me. Mac pulled out his makings and rolled a tight little cigarette. It was the one thing he did that brought Glory immediately to mind—their hands matched. Them rolling cigarettes was exactly the same: the same flick of the wrist, the same fluffing of tobacco, the same quick tongue darting out to wet the glue on the paper.

We watched the fire. I felt the heat coming off Bud's great big body and I leaned into him. Bud looked up at Mac and said over the sound of the fire, "That place down the bay, the Chance cabin, you know who's got it now?"

Mac shook his head. Took a drag.

"A Chance, again. Danny. Youngest grandson of old man Chance. Lucky son-of-a... Excuse me. Lucky fellow, walking into that setup."

Mac raised his eyebrows.

"He's working at the mill, on my shift. Nice guy. Got a wife and a baby. Though, the wife, she's not too happy here..." He trailed off.

This sounded familiar. "I met the wife," I said.

"Did you?"

"Outside the pub. Yesterday, walking with the baby." I remembered her pretty brown eyes watching me and Glory spit fire, her skinny jeans, her city clothes.

They looked at me like, carry on, but I wouldn't. A portion of the fire collapsed in on itself and sparks shot up to the treetops.

"I worry about Danny," Bud went on. "He's dumb as a newborn calf, in a way. Don't know nothing about this place, but there's something to him. He's alright."

Mac nodded and looked toward the kitchen window. I followed his eyes and we watched Juniper bob around the kitchen. She was dancing, lit up like Christmas and us all watching. Mac and I shared a smile. Juniper poured the kettle of boiled water carefully into the teapot. Mac stubbed out his cigarette on the porch and nudged Bud with his knee. We rose to go in, but on the threshold, I couldn't. Bud and Mac looked at me, then Mac turned and went in. He shut the door after him.

"What is it?" Bud came in close.

"I don't know. I don't want to come out of the wind, I guess."

Bud looked out toward the lake. It was black and loud, pounding the rocky beach. "You wanna stay out here?" He looked into the house, at the warm light pouring out of the window.

"Come down to the water," I said to him.

He grabbed a blanket from his truck and put it around me. I led him down the rickety stairs to the shore and, once down there, talking was pointless against the noise of the water. I opened the blanket and pulled him in. He put his arm around me and we walked that way, bumping hips and tripping over rocks, toward the point.

Nights like that, with the wind and the waves, you feel the weight of the lake. Like someone else's shadow following behind you. It's always there, like a bogeyman. It was hard not to think about all the people lost on the lake. Glory's other brother, Alfred, Anton's twin, died when they were teenagers. Drunk boating. Like so many boys dredged out or washed up onshore, dead. Nobody ever talked about Alfred anymore. If there's a superstitious connection between everyone in this town, it's that we don't talk about the lake dead. It hurts too much. And you never know if you're next.

My shivering started up again, thinking that stuff, as we walked. Bud pulled me in tight and stopped me once we were past Swannells' and almost to the point. He pulled the blanket over our heads so we were in a little tent out of the wind. I thought he was going to try to kiss me again.

"Crystal, I wanna tell you something." He paused. His breath was hot on my cheek. "Look, this doesn't mean nothing to me. I mean, it means a lot to me. I've been waiting a long time..."

"I know," I said.

"I don't think you know all of it."

"What?" I didn't want to talk. I could smell his deodorant and the spicier smell of him underneath it. I leaned in and pressed my nose to his neck.

"Crystal, I can't do this if it don't mean the same to you. I need this to matter and I'm telling you, if we start this up again it's not going to finish."

I laughed. "Is that a threat?"

He took my jaw in one hand and held my face so it was in line with his, though neither of us could see the other.

"It's a promise. I mean it, Crystal."

There was a steeliness to his voice and I bristled, but there was a backbone in that promise I wanted. I'd never had it before, and there were times when Glory was on a bender in Prince George or Burns Lake when it all went bad and there was no one but me to get us out of danger and into our own beds. I wanted someone to make sure I got home safe, too.

I stood on my tiptoes and leaned into Bud's hand, hoping his mouth was where I thought it was. My lips met his moustache and I shivered again, pushed in harder, found his mouth, and kissed him. He let go of my jaw and pulled me close.

"Yes," I said, in the fug of the blanket tent, once we'd separated to breathe. That was a promise, too.

I pulled the screen door open and let him in like a gentleman. Bud allowed it, but I knew he wouldn't next time. I grinned at him and he leaned in to smooch me again, but I pushed him through the door instead. I wanted to watch him discover Mac's place.

The room was like falling into the lake, like coming up for air after you jumped in off the cliff and went deep, like you'd dived in so far you were bursting for air, the bubbles streaming past you. But then you realize right away you can breathe and it's just an illusion. Every wall was blue or green or grey or black, hung with cloth cut and stitched together in sharp angles, so it became obvious this was the lake, quilted and hung, like it had been mounted mid-wave. Still water, storm, underwater, on the water, sky and water, it was all there, almost moving. I watched Bud plant his feet wide so he could look without getting seasick: quilts as big as walls between the windows. I let him look, then I shoved him from behind and laughed at him.

"Guess I didn't warn you, eh?"

He just stared.

"Got some tea, guys," Juniper said. She put a mug in my hands and the steam rose and warmed my face. I gave the mug to Bud and went in close to my favourite quilt. Most of them were made of wool and flannel scraps. There was cotton, worn-out cotton, some of it stained in spots, most of it white or blue, but my favourite was made of a dress I could remember my auntie wearing: cornflowers so thick no ground showed, and no sky, either. I stroked the flowers with the tip of my finger. Up close it was like shattered glass—all triangles and straight lines—the lake broken up and seen through cracked eyeglasses. But when I turned and looked at the quilt across the room I could make out a boat, a grey boat, next to dark cliffs, one of them with a hole right through.

Chance point. The town a brown smear off to the right.

"Pretty neat, hey?"

Bud took a sip of milky orange pekoe. I went and sat with Juniper on the couch. I watched him do a double take when he looked at us. I knew what he saw: it was like me and Glory in high school, except it wasn't Glory—short hair and no sneer—and I was old and wrinkly. And tired. I let myself sink into the cushions, ready to weep after the day I'd had, all the emotions still roiling so close to my surface.

Mac came in and smiled at us there on the couch.

Bud said, "Mr. Stuart, these quilts are something else."

Juniper said, "They're made of Nana's leftovers. Sheets and blankets and clothes. Some of it he got from the second-hand store, but mostly it's Nana's. She had a lot of blue stuff."

I said, "He taught himself. He was mending Juniper's stuff, anyway, and when she went to bed, well, there's no TV out here, so he sewed."

Mac shrugged. He put down his tea and cracked the lid on a Crock-Pot on the counter. Yellow steam rose and the smell of ham and peas escaped. The phone rang and Juniper got up to answer it.

"Papa!"

My guts dropped. I knew instantly something was wrong.

Anton and Tiny hadn't come in from fishing. It was Tiny's wife on the phone. They were talking search and rescue. I looked out the window and tears started up in my eyes. Not Anton. Not Tiny. Not my cousins, because then it was also me. And Glory. We'd lost too many neighbours and friends and Alfred... I looked at Mac. These were his boys. His eyes were shut. I took his arm.

"Mac, what do you want us to do?"

His voice was rough. "Go get Glory. Keep her safe."

"That's all? Shouldn't we bring her here?" Bud asked.

"She's going to lose it when she finds out. She'll go nuts and we don't know what she'll do. We can't bring her here, though. She doesn't come here." I turned back to Mac. "I'll find her," I said. I hugged him, and he was like a bird whose feathers compress when you pick it up in your hands. I held him for a second too long and then I turned to Bud. "I've gotta go."

"I'll come, too."

I shook my head. "I need to tell her alone. She's going to want to go after them or burn shit down, I don't even know."

He was confused. "But you might need me."

"Of course I need you," I snapped, "but not like that. You need to see if you can help with search and rescue or something." I swallowed. All of us knew how stories like this ended up: coffins and wakes, not search and rescue. "Bud?" I held his arm. "I need your truck." I was wrecking it, I could tell. He wouldn't understand. I wanted to throw up.

But instead of pushing me down or walking away, he fished out his truck keys and handed them to me.

"It's a stiff clutch. Let it out slow. Crystal..." He couldn't get it out.

I didn't want to watch him try, so I interrupted. "I know," I said. "Me, too."

As I left, Juniper was crying into the phone.

CHORUS

Leah Janine Anderson, outside the high school

This town's a motherfucker. You get born here, you live for a while, you grow and go to school and eat and drink and party, maybe you even get married and have babies, and then you die.

I hate the assholes who move away and then move back. What the hell is wrong with them? Why'd they move away in the first place if they're only gonna come back? I bet I know. I been thinking about it. They got nothing more to prove here. Everyone knows how great they were when they were young and partied hard. But everyone knows all their fuck-ups, too. Can't get away from it here. Even their kids will grow up knowing all the sucky ways they fucked up when they were young. In your own hometown you're sort of famous, though. And that's something. You got a light?

I heard about a girl here who was going to be famous for real, outside of Fort. I heard she was this great musician who was going to play in California or Hollywood or somewhere, and then something bad happened and she never went. Someone said she was that one who sings at the pub, but I don't believe them. She's too old and she's ugly. She doesn't sing good, either. My uncle says she could sing like kite strings, whatever that means. I think he meant like an angel. I heard that before. But I think he meant the other one—there are two of them, sisters or cousins. That one only whores around. I heard that, too. You hear everything in a small town.

Cousins, probably. That's not hard to believe—everyone is your cousin here. My aunt had ten kids, so I have lots of cousins. I hate some of them, too. Some of them are real assholes.

I go to school with that one's daughter. No one says she's her daughter, but lots of people know Juniper was raised by someone else because her mother was busy singing and whoring. And Juniper? She's smarter than anyone in my school. She'll get scholarships and she'll get out of here. I might, too, because I'm good at volleyball, even though I'm not real tall. So, there's a good chance I'll leave, but Juniper, she'll go, and she'll go far. No one's worried about her.

I worry about me, though. If I'll get out for real. You hear so many stories about kids with big hopes and kids with talent who fuck it up, or get knocked up, or die in the lake before they can go. I'm real careful when I hear a story like that. I wear a life jacket in a boat and I make my boyfriend wear a condom even though he hates them. I try hard at school, but I'll never be as good as Juniper. But if I were Juniper, I'd work hard, too, coming from that mother and all those stories about her.

CRYSTAL

I retraced the drunk journey I'd walked earlier that day. My heart ached when I remembered the shit I'd said to Glory over breakfast.

I drove the five kilometres to the pub in silence, struggling with the truck—its high cab and man-shaped seat and gears made me stretch and lurch; I had to almost stand on the clutch to downshift.

The pub's parking lot was packed—junky cars and skooked-up pickups, a semi with no trailer, naked-looking, butted up right to the front door. Somebody's idea of a joke: parking like a maniac. I wanted to see if she'd come into town before I headed all the way out to her place. The pub was a likely spot.

I walked in. The night was rocking: a tree-planting crew had taken over the whole pool-table side and a game of full-contact pool was underway. Sandy had jugs lined up on the bar for Lou-Ellen to deliver, but Lou-Ellen was stuck talking to a man in low-riding jeans who had her pinned against the wall near the toilets. I could see her trying to squeeze her tray under his arm to get away. The TV was on over the mantel and two tables were shouting at a hockey game. I was scanning the pub for Glory but my eyes stopped at the bar—a familiar back, ball cap, low-hanging head. Hardy.

Shit. I knew Hardy was likely to know where Glory was, but I didn't want to talk to him. Oh God, I didn't want to.

I made my legs move, anyway, and sidled up to the bar. Sandy was there in a flash.

"You want anything?" she said to me, her eyes gobbling up the gossip of us. "Another, Hardy?"

Hardy took one look at her and she scooted off.

Hardy looked at me sideways. Straightened his back. Pushed his ball cap back on his head.

"You seen Glory tonight, Hardy?"

Hardy narrowed his eyes. "What's it to you?" He turned his body away from me. "What the hell do you want?"

"Just looking for her on behalf of her dad." That was strange enough for me to say that he turned back. Everyone knew Mac Stuart had nothing to say to his daughter. "I have to tell her something and I don't know where she is."

He made me wait a long beat. "Why should I tell you where she is?"

I didn't know the answer to that. I knew why anyone else should tell me where she was: they'd care that I was freaking out. Hardy didn't care. He went back to his beer.

"Her brothers are on the lake. They didn't come in from fishing."

He took a sip of beer. The conversation was over, as far as he was concerned. But I wasn't done. Around us the talk and the laughter swirled, but eyes were on us, I could feel them.

"Fuck you, Hardy."

A chill went through me. Sound slipped away as I watched him for some reaction, some snake strike, venom and muscle, but he only paused before he sipped again.

I turned to go, then I heard him say, soft, "I haven't seen her tonight."

I looked back, and in the mirror behind the bar I could see his eyes on me. They were still and mean and they said: fuck you.

It was a dark ride out to Southside. The wind threw branches across the road and trees leaned drunkenly over the pavement. I parked in the driveway and walked down the root-lumpy path through the cottonwoods toward the light I could see through the trees. Then I noticed the music. I stopped for a second. Pink Floyd. That didn't sound like Glory.

"As if you never party here," I said, as if she could hear me.

A bottle smashed and laughter rose over the music. I started running.

From the outside, with the lights on, it looked like a carousel. People moved behind the blurry window screens, flickered, their shadows falling on the ground outside in dizzying patterns. I heard another laugh, then saw a hand press onto the window, palm out, perfect and dainty. Glory's, I was sure. I lunged for the door.

It was Renee Chance, with her back to me, dancing with her arms out. I was confused—it had looked like the shack was full of people, but it was empty except for Renee and the music blasting out of the ripped speaker. I pulled the cord from the wall and my ears popped in the sudden silence. Renee whipped around. She brought her arms down as if she was nude, trying to cover her body. Then she put one hand on her hip and ran the other through her hair.

"Where's Glory?" I walked further into the shack, pushing empty bottles off the table in a show of ownership.

"She's gone. Her boyfriend came this afternoon and they left. I think they drove into town." She sat on a bench with her bony fingers in her lap. She had bags under her eyes. She sat, hunched, and chewed a cuticle.

"Her boyfriend?" I dropped onto the bench nearest me.

"Some guy with floppy hair. He had nice teeth."

Oh, fuck. "Todd."

"That's it. She said she wanted to go somewhere new and he said he wanted to go somewhere old and so they left."

"Why didn't you go?"

"I didn't want to go anywhere."

"Well, you're coming with me. We've gotta find them. Glory's brothers are out on the lake and she's gonna freak out when she hears about it. Best she hears it from me." I stood up, but Renee didn't move. "Well?"

She didn't so much lie down on the bench as fold into herself. It was pitiful. Tears and snot leaked out of her face.

I grabbed her by the arm. "Oh, for fucksake. Get up! This isn't about you. People are in danger and we've got to help."

"What can I do?"

"You can quit feeling sorry for yourself."

She must have been scared of me because she got up. She put on the sweater of Glory's I threw at her and slid her feet into her shoes. I grabbed a sweater myself and a box of granola bars. I was shaky with hunger. "Get going." I marched her out the door. "The truck's just up here."

Bud's truck started up fine. Renee got in and slammed the door, and I jammed my foot onto the clutch, put it in reverse, and backed it up onto the road and started toward town. I didn't know how to work the stereo or the heater. Our breath steamed up the windows and I had to crack mine so it didn't fog up so much I couldn't see. Outside, Fort St. James rolled past, quiet and deceiving, all its wounds bound up from sight but flowing deadly and silent from unseen sores. Over the bridge, past the public works yard, past the slough and creek, past the boarded-up gas station. A dog trundled out in front of me just a few houses into the reserve, and I stood on the brakes. It didn't even look our way, but its buddy did, teeth in a grin that glinted in the headlights.

Glory would have laughed at me. She always told me to wait for the second dog.

Renee was crying softly in the front seat. "Where are we going, anyway? Are we going to the police station?"

"No. We have to find her ourselves." I glanced at her and felt some pity starting up. "I could take you home."

She panicked. "No! You can't. I mean, don't. I mean, I can't." Then she gave up and just kept crying.

I remembered Renee had a kid. "Where's your baby?"

She sniffled. "With his dad."

"Are you still with him?"

She didn't answer. She wiped her eyes with the arm of the sweater.

I couldn't help, so I didn't say anything. I peered through the dark at the empty streets and quiet houses and the lake churning beyond them.

"I can't imagine being out in that," she said eventually.

"Try not to," I said. "Most of us spend our living days trying not to imagine what it'd be like to drown in there."

"That's pretty morbid."

I shrugged.

"Don't you have happy memories of the lake?"

"Yeah," I said. I did. Me and Glory all sticky with Popsicles, walking up and down Cottonwood Beach in our bikinis when the summers were so long they had no end; me and Glory driving with all the windows open when the northern lights were glowing green-tiger stripes right down to the ground; swimming out at Southside when her mom and my mom were only sisters and neither one was dead. "Yeah, I've got memories."

"You should try and dwell on those."

"Don't tell me what to do. You have no idea." I breathed in deep. I let the anger go out with my breath, away with the wind. I heard her snuffle. I turned to look at her in the patchy light and she seemed so small and shabby. God. "I'm sorry. I just get mad."

"Screw you."

"What?" That surprised me.

"Don't apologize because you pity me. I don't need your pity."

"Jesus. Fine." I looked away from her. "Look, I don't know your story and you don't know mine. Neither of us knows what in fuck we're doing here, but it looks like we're stuck together until we find Glory. They're not going to find those boys tonight. The best thing we can do is just find her and keep her safe." However safe she could be with Todd, I thought. "Help me figure out where to go. She wanted to go somewhere new and what did he want? To go somewhere old? We'll try the fort. That's the oldest place in town."

I took a left after the fry shack at the edge of the reserve. We pulled into the service lot at the fort. A lawn tractor was parked in the grass by the fence. Beyond the fence, the silver wood of the buildings shone in the street lights, the rest of the compound in darkness. I parked the truck and we sat there for a moment. I heard the truck tick and ping.

"Where are we?" Renee asked, staring out the windshield.

"Historic fort," I said. Anyone from here wouldn't need more of an explanation, but she looked confused. "It's the Hudson's Bay Fort. Kind of a museum." I thought of Bud reading in the archives, wherever those were. It made me smile to think of him hunkered over old books. "They redid it in the seventies. Brought the old broken-down buildings up to 1880s standards and rebuilt other buildings from pictures. It's a national park now."

We got out of the truck and walked up to the tall fence. I slipped a rope latch over the top of a fence post and opened a gate.

"Shouldn't it be harder to get into if it's a national park?" Renee asked.

"It usually is. In the daytime. This is the service entrance. Maybe there's no night watchman? Besides, who'd want to come out in this to check the grounds?" I pushed through the gate, walked through a dark garden, and out another gate onto the grounds, Renee right on my heels. The wind smashed into us as soon as we left the last gate. Boardwalks crossed the grass ahead and seemed to break off suddenly when the street lights ran out.

Where was Glory? I didn't know my way around the fort. I hadn't been there since grade school, but it wasn't big—the entire thing seemed to be laid out in a square in front of us: four buildings connected by the boardwalk, the wild lake out front, a flagpole, and many, many flat brown shapes on the lawns.

"What are those?" Renee asked, leaning over.

"Cow shit, I think." I looked around for the culprit prowling around in the night, but saw nothing. Then I heard Glory laugh. "Over here!" I grabbed Renee's hand and pulled. We ran down the boardwalk toward the biggest building.

Renee put her hand on the wooden wall while I peered into the dark beyond it. "I didn't know this place was here. I bet it's amazing in the light."

I glanced around at the shadowy fences and the blocky buildings and remembered how silvery they were in daytime. "Yeah, it is, kind of."

"What was this building, do you think?"

"The fur warehouse. Maybe. I think Grade 4 was the last time I was here. They stored the furs here before they shipped them out. That's about all I know of Canadian history. I know it was a party place before Parks Canada took it over. My dad told me stories about riding bikes off the pier."

There was constant movement all around us: the long grasses from last summer rustled in the wind; the building creaked and settled; the trees around the fort rattled and banged, their branches whipping back and forth.

"I wonder if Danny knows about this place."

"Your husband? He would. I heard he's a Chance."

"Jesus, this is a small town."

"Ain't that the truth. This is a tourist place. He probably visited when he was a kid."

Renee looked around, maybe trying to see the place differently from Danny's having been there when he was small, but how could she? It was dark. There was just the wind and the water eating away the shore. We walked to the front of the building and I tried the door. It didn't budge. I rattled the huge metal handle.

"Hey, Crystal, do you know what happened with Danny's granddad? I know there's something."

That made me pause. I asked her, "You don't know?" There were probably reasons I shouldn't tell her, but I didn't care. Maybe she was entitled to know. "They say he killed his wife." I glanced at her and saw the whites of her eyes. "He may have. He may have killed his wife, that's what they say. I know he lived on that point where you live and he and his neighbour Swannell worked up here in the bush for years. Forty years, maybe more? My uncle Mac said they cleared this whole area. They were partners."

"But what about his wife?"

"I think Chance had it harder than Swannell. Swannell was younger. He and his wife worked their piece of land together. But Chance's wife was sick. And his boys were wild. Mean. You still hear stories about them. Mrs. Chance had cerebral palsy or something. Chance couldn't look after her like she needed. I don't know why she wasn't in the hospital." I led Renee around the lake side of the building and the wind took our breath. We ducked back to the building's front and crowded into the doorway.

"Mrs. Chance got really sick and then no one saw her again. We heard she died, but there was something about the way she died wasn't right. They said that Chance did it. No one blamed him totally—she was sick and suffering—but he was never part of the town again after that. He cut himself off. Even from Swannell.

"Their sons left, then one of them came back with the little boys—Danny and his brother—once or twice, but then never again. Danny's moving back surprised everyone."

"But what happened to his granddad?"

I watched her for a second. "He killed himself."

"How?"

"The lake."

She held herself tightly, arms wrapped around her elbows. "And how did he kill his wife?"

"They say the bathtub, but I don't believe it. He probably smothered her."

"Why didn't he go to jail?"

"I don't know. Maybe he should have. But maybe he did her a favour."

She was quiet. I thought about her bathtub. The bed, the walls, everything about that cabin had probably changed because of what I told her. "I'm sorry. Did I wreck it for you?"

"What?" She seemed dazed.

"Your place."

"No," she said, and let out her breath. "I feel like you... fixed it for me."

My turn: "What?"

"Maybe that's all it is—maybe it's the place that feels helpless and sad. I felt so trapped all winter. It was dark so early and it was always cold in there, even when I had the fire blazing I felt cold. Now, I'm thinking about the bedroom. Maybe it wasn't really awful to be in bed with Danny. Maybe it's something the house projected. Is that ridiculous?"

It was, but I didn't say so. I sort of half nodded. It was probably pretty creepy to live there.

"I remember this night last winter, when Thomas wouldn't sleep. He cried every time I tried to lay him down. At one point, all three of us were in one chair, rocking, all of us staring out at the water, all exhausted, like we'd washed up from a shipwreck on an island while everyone in the world was asleep. It was amazing. It was the only time I ever felt like that—a little family, alone against the world. The rest of the time it's been awful." She paused. "What do people say about the cabin?" she asked.

I told her: that it's haunted. That Chance was unlucky. That the bay is unlucky because of him. "But it wasn't just Chance who was unlucky. Swannell and his wife couldn't have any kids. And she taught kindergarten. She loved kids. Glory and I were in her class and she always let us sit together. And it's a beautiful bay. They get the best sunsets in the world over there. They say the fishing's good, too. There's no curse. I think people curse themselves repeating that stuff. They just want to feel better off than someone else. Chance couldn't help the hand he was dealt. None of us can."

We leaned against the door and let the wind blow away everything I said. I heard the waves crashing and Renee snuffling again.

"You okay?"

"Danny said I can't come back."

"Did he mean it?"

"I don't know. I think so."

"That why you went to Glory?"

"I had nowhere else to go. She's the only friend I have in town."

That made me pause—it was true for both of us. What in hell did that mean?

"Maybe Danny's not so mad."

"He kicked me out. I'd say he's pretty mad."

We stood there in the dark together and I realized neither one of us had a real anchor. We'd both clung to Glory, but she was hardly solid. And now we didn't even know where she was. I felt sick and lost, and if I felt sick and lost, Renee probably felt worse—she'd lost her family. I shifted closer so our hips touched and we shared that small warmth in the night.

"What do you want to do?" I asked her eventually.

"Go back to when Danny loved me and I loved him. Figure out how to be a mom, how to be okay." She hauled in a deep breath and let it out.

"I want to go back to when things were simple, when it was just me and Glory singing," I said.

"Don't you have anyone else? A boyfriend?"

"I do now, I guess."

"If you went back in time you'd lose him."

"That might happen, anyway."

"Pretty fatalistic way of thinking about things."

I shrugged. "Shit happens. That's a guarantee."

"But if shit happens, then love happens. Even if you lose it, you'll get it again."

"I like your logic." I smiled at her even if she couldn't see me. Maybe she wasn't as bad as I'd thought. "I guess that's true for you, too, isn't it?"

I could hear her smile back. "I hope so."

A smashed can landed at my feet and made me jump. Glory landed there right after. She was zipping up her fly.

"Hey! It's Crystal! Where have you been?" She stood up and brushed off her butt. She walked over with her arms out to hug me, I thought, but then she swung her fist at me.

I grabbed her. "You're drunk."

"So what? That's for this morning. You were drunk when you left. Aren't you drunk anymore? Is that what's wrong? You want a drink?"

"Shut up, Glory."

"I got drinks if that's what you want. We're having a party!"

Todd moseyed out of the dark, doing up the buttons on his coat, all handsome and smarmy.

"You can have a drink if you want one. We got beer."

I opened my mouth to tell her, but it wouldn't come. Tears came instead.

"What, for fucksake?" She pushed me away.

"Glory," I managed, but it came out funny. "Anton and Tiny are out on the lake."

"What are they doing on the lake? It's night."

"They're lost or they ran out of gas or something. They went out today and they're still out there."

"No. Anton wouldn't stay out after dark. No. They're not on the lake. They're probably at the pub."

"The police called. They said they're sending out search and rescue."

"They're at the pub! They're just at the pub. Or the Cab. Check there!"

"I came from the pub—they're not there."

She pushed past me and ran toward the lake. Todd stood with a stupid look; Renee knew nothing about this place, these people, what mattered—neither of them moved. I tore after her.

There was just light enough to see the white crests on the water and the dark blob of Glory against the water. She was already coming back up toward me.

"How'd you get here," she yelled. "You got a truck?"

I had her figured, so I bodychecked her and pinned her down. She fought me, sobbing and scratching.

"Let me go! We've gotta get them! We'll get a boat!"

"We can't go out in a storm, you know that." I held her tight.

"What are we going to do?"

"I'm going to keep you safe, like Mac said."

Glory bucked under me. "Mac didn't say that. He doesn't care about me."

"He does, too," I said.

"Shut up, Crystal. You're a traitor and a bitch." She squirmed to get out from under me, but I held on. She went slack all of a sudden, the fight leaking out of her. Her arms snaked around me and I hugged her back. The night fell around us like a song we'd written when we were drunk and high, full of stars and wind, less about something than the feeling of something. I couldn't feel my own heartbeat for the pounding of hers. It wasn't the first time I'd held her like a scared little sister, but it felt like the most important time.

"Is it true they're out there?" she asked. "They were fishing?"

"Yeah. Tiny's wife called."

"Were you at Mac's?"

I nodded into her shoulder.

"I wish you wouldn't go there."

"I can't help it."

"How is she?" She meant Juniper.

"Big. It was her answered the phone."

"Of course it was. She's grown-up."

"Yeah, for ten."

"I hate this town."

"I know you do."

"Don't leave me."

"You know I won't." Don't leave me, I thought.

The wind threw down cottonwood catkins at us and bits of branch and leaves. Glory sat up and I let her. I lay where I was and watched her sway. She was drunk. Her eyes darted around and her hair moved like a horse's mane in the wind. She watched the lake. She said, "I can't even remember

Alfred, you know that? I can't call up his face. I can't remember anything we ever did together. I hate myself for that. I think, how can I love Anton like I do and I can't even remember his twin. My own brother."

"It happened a long time ago. You were just a kid." I didn't touch her because I knew not to. If I touched her, she would leave. If I stayed quiet, she'd keep talking. She picked up a cottonwood fluff and started flaking it apart. But I couldn't not talk. "Alfred was smaller than Anton, right?" I hardly remembered him.

"Smaller, but just a little bit. He had lighter hair. Anton could pick him up and chuck him around. They used to wrestle."

"I remember that," I said. And I could, a little. Something about a lawn and two big boys on it, grown men on the porch cooking burgers. A summer night. "I don't remember why he was on the lake, though."

"He wasn't supposed to be," she said. "He snuck out onto Chuck Dodd's boat one time when they were having a party. He was younger than everyone else, but they let him go along. They went out to the diving rocks past Sowchea to go cliff jumping. Alfred jumped from way high up and when he hit the water he lost his bearings. Fuck. I hate that. I hate the picture in my head of him swimming toward the bottom. I can just see it. It's so quiet and blue and he's thrashing to get there faster, except he's swimming down instead of to the surface."

"I remember the service at the Friendship Centre."

"I hate that place," she said. She threw the cotton at the wind but it blew away from us, back toward the trees. She looked like a mermaid—her jeans could have been a tail, her white skin and long hair, her face wet with tears.

"Let's get the fuck out of here. All the beer is gone. We can't help them, so let's get drunk." It was awful, but just like her: mean, so she wasn't vulnerable; crass and foul-mouthed, so it didn't show she was hurt.

I hauled her up the bank, onto the boardwalk, and she grabbed on so tight it was hard to walk. Todd sauntered over, and Glory dropped me and reached for him. Also typical. I tried not to care. We started back toward the service entrance and the truck, pushed on by the wind. I felt a tug at my shirt. It was Renee. I reached back for her hand, gave it a squeeze, and pulled her along. I could do that, at least.

CHORUS
Allan James, historic fort caretaker,
campfire, Paarens Beach

No one sings folk songs about the Siberia of the fur trade,
Fort St. James. Maybe around the fire, men sang songs of
old Caledonia and conjured memories over the flames, but
when the winter closed in there was no place for song. They
ate dried salmon day and night, the wind blew, and still
there were chores: water to haul, tools to repair, company
business to attend to, and at night, no women to offer them
comfort. There was no family to draw near.

The Hudson's Bay Company sent men here to the far
west to prove themselves loyal, or to sort themselves out;
Fort St. James was the end of the known world, and its in-
hospitable climate did the work of punishment and man-
making all at once. They came back east chagrined, stalwart,
or stark raving mad. Trading furs out west, at the mercy of
the Carrier people, who kept them in salmon and taught
them to live on the shore of a lake that would as soon flay
them as feed them. This made something of them—not
men, not workers loyal to the cause—it humbled them, it
made them kneel. And a kneeling man is either subservient
or spent. It's hard to tell which at a glance.

Three times the Fort burned down. Three times the men
were out of doors in the middle of winter. Did they curse
the blaze Simon Fraser scraped into a tree with his axe in
the middle of the wilderness in 1806? Samuel MacGuire
shot an eagle out of the sky on Christmas day. Once the
Carrier were gone for a full year, no word from them, and

then they were back. By then, two parties had set out to find game. Only one returned.

The men made the Carrier move their village. They built a church with little houses around it, like a mother hen and her chicks. That burned down, too, once or twice. There must have been years without fire. The records are incomplete. Imagine the northern lights like green flames in the sky, reaching down the to earth, then withdrawing.

They caught salmon and dried salmon and kept it in the fish cache the Carrier helped them build. They built a stockade, but took it down once they realized their dependence on their nomadic neighbours. They bore the brunt of the weather that built up the length of the lake and wracked whatever shelter they constructed on its shore. They died and were replaced. They traded fur, packaged fur, sent out fur on mule trains, and waited for the ice to go out in the spring. They built a schooner to get them out to Babine Portage and to bring the goods back in. They developed the Carrier's dependence on their goods: hard tack, flour, nails, and booze. There was an awful cost for the booze. Boots, hobnails, squat stoves, and blankets, coloured stripes on them like blood streaked on snow.

They left behind buildings with dovetailed corners, stairways that creaked in the shifts of weather, walls chinked with manure and straw. They papered the Men's House with advertisements for women's corsets. They waited all winter for mail. They built boardwalks to keep themselves out of the mud and shit in the spring. They fixed gutters to the fur warehouse. They shot bears creeping round the fish cache, and missed, or not. The shot is still embedded in the corner post. See? They built post-on-sill, they lived as well as they could, and they ate the dogs one New Year's when they ran out of salmon. Did they sing? There's no record of that. There are no surviving folk songs from the Siberia of the fur trade.

PART THREE

A Story They Tell at the Bar

DANNY

The knock on the door scared the shit out of me. Thomas, too—he started crying. I picked him up and went to answer it. I knew it wouldn't be Renee, she wouldn't knock, but even so, my heart hammered in my throat. I flung open the door, angry that just the thought of her could make me so weak.

Bud stood in the porchlight with his hair plastered over his forehead, hunched up against the wind. I must've looked surprised, because he laughed at me. "Hey, Dan. Mind if I come in?"

"No! No, of course not. Come in." I got out of his way. I put Thomas in his high chair and strapped him in so I could take Bud's coat. "Wild night to be out."

He headed straight for the wood stove once he got his boots off. He rubbed his hands together, nodding, but I could see that something was off. "Nice place, Dan. Cozy."

I put the kettle on, opting for hot toddies instead of beer, choosing for Bud because I could see he was still deciding how to tell me why he was here. My heart thudded. I couldn't think of another reason for him to be here except for Renee. But if something had happened to her, the cops would have been here, too. So Bud wasn't here about Renee. He didn't know she'd left and he didn't know where she was and he wasn't a messenger from her. I knew all that. I tried to calm myself, getting out mugs and rum and cinnamon, but I was sweating.

"You going to tell me why you're here, Bud?"

"Jeez, Dan, I'm sorry. I was just over at Mac Stuart's. You know him? He's just down the bay there, past the Swannells'. There's a real bad thing going on tonight. His boys are out in this." He included the lake, the weather, the night, in his nod at the window. "I want to help, but there's nothing to do. I don't have my truck, so I couldn't go, but I couldn't stay at Mac's, either. The Swannells are over there, now, and the police are on their way."

I looked out the window and shook my head. What was there to say? "I'm sorry, Bud. That's terrible." Thomas was squawking, so I picked up his stacking toy and put it on the tray. I touched his soft hair. "What did you say about your truck? Who took it?"

Bud blushed. "Crystal." He swallowed, looked away. "She went to find Glory Stuart, to let her know about her brothers."

The name made me seethe. I went back to the kettle, poured rum into the mugs, and added hot water, lemon juice, a cinnamon stick, clenching my teeth, replaying the fight with Renee in my head.

"Dan? You okay?" Bud had come up beside me. He took one of the mugs.

"Renee left. I mean, I kicked her out. She said she was leaving, and she said she was going with Glory, so I don't know. There can't be two Glorys, right? Maybe they're already gone."

Bud put his hand on my arm, just above my elbow, and squeezed. It was a strange, manly gesture, and it almost broke me. I took a breath. Bud went to sit at the table near the high chair. Thomas offered him the red plastic doughnut he'd been whacking on his tray and Bud took it.

He didn't ask any more, but I told him about Renee, about the winter we'd spent in silence, and about the previous night, when she hadn't come home. I had to stop a couple times, to really breathe so I wouldn't lose it, but Bud understood. He traded colourful doughnuts with Thomas and sipped his drink. When I was done, he set his doughnut down and shook his head.

"That's hard, Dan. I don't know anything harder than trying to keep things together when one of you's bent on leaving."

I shook my head. "Mac Stuart's facing something harder. I haven't got it so bad as all that." I stood up. "You want another?"

"Nah. Listen, Dan. I don't know what we can do, but I think we should try and do something. Crystal's gone to find Glory, and I know how that's going to go." He rolled his eyes. "But whatever goes on with them, I think they'll end up at the pub. And I think I should be there. Would you be willing to give me a ride? I know it's a lot to ask." He looked at Thomas, who was trying not to fall asleep on his toys.

"Sure, Bud. I'll do that. Maybe I can get the Swannells to watch Thomas. He's just going to go to sleep. They can keep an eye on him while they're staying with Mac."

"I'd appreciate your help, and I know Mac would, too. You haven't met, have you?"

"Maybe, when I was a kid. I don't remember a lot from back then."

We got Thomas bundled up, packed up the playpen, and headed out on foot to Stuart's. I thought it would be easier to walk over than to drive all the way out to the road and then double back down the driveway in the car, but the wind was worse than I thought. We walked the path Renee had beaten between the houses. In the clearing near the Swannells' carport, the wind was so fierce, it howled through the trees and tore at our clothes. I had Thomas tucked inside a blanket and held him tight to me. His toque was down over his eyes. He didn't like it and fussed. I paused in the lee of the Swannells' porch to fix it.

Bud came up beside me. "Stuart's is just over there." He pointed at the next house down the bay. It was hidden behind a stand of trees, but I could see lights blazing from every window. I looked at the path between the houses and I felt like I'd been here before. I must have, since I remembered rambling all over the bay when I was a kid, but I had a feeling about this path. A memory tugged at me.

Bud led the way, hauling the playpen, and I followed, Thomas complaining in my ear. I was sure I knew this place, and when we pushed through the trees and into the driveway, I knew I was right. I'd been here before, and it had been a night like this.

I was thirteen the last time my dad had brought us up here from Vancouver. My brother was ten. He was after something, my dad—we only came back when he was broke or on the run. I remember he was drunk, shouting at my granddad. Jimmy was asleep, but I couldn't stand it. I put on my coat and took off out the back door. I remember feeling like I couldn't breathe if I faced the water, where the wind ripped the air right out of my mouth. I found a path through the trees and followed it, first to the Swannells'—I knew them, they were neighbours—but then I carried on past their house, down another path, to another little, grey, hip-roofed house in the trees.

I thought it was abandoned. No lights were on. I went around the back, away from the wind, and stepped up onto the veranda. There was a chair at either end, and I slumped in the near one. A girl's voice startled me.

"You don't wait for an invitation, do you?"

I jumped, but didn't run. More curious than embarrassed, I wanted to know who she was. I didn't think there were other kids on the bay. She was smoking, and she told me her parents were asleep inside. She didn't know who I was or what my problem was, but she saw I had one, and instead of sending me packing, she said, "Come on," and led me back to my granddad's property.

I remember she wore a mackinaw jacket, man-sized, and gumboots—she was bundled up, and I wished I was, too. She offered me her toque, even went so far as to pull it off her head and hold it out to me, but I wouldn't take it. Her long, curly black hair blew around in the wind. She was exactly my height. We were standing behind a bush and I was close enough to kiss her.

"This way." She had a flashlight. She led me over the point, past the gazebo my granddad had built that had been falling down since my grandmother died. She crouched, and we made our way down a steep rock face on a ledge just wide enough for us to walk single file. The water was close, splashing up the cliff at us, but she didn't hesitate. She reached back for my hand and pulled me into a cave in the rock just big enough for two.

"You didn't know this was here, did you?" She tucked us both in so we were facing out at the lake. The waves swallowed the lights of the far shore, then spat them out again. We looked out at the water, and she said, "Sometimes I come here to cry. It's private. I bet we're the only two who know about this place, now. I think someone else used to use it, once upon a time. I found ashes from a little fire the first time I came here." She looked at my face. She used her sleeve to wipe the water from my cheeks. "Now, what are you crying about tonight?"

"I'm not crying. That's rain."

"It's windy, but it isn't raining."

I didn't know what to say. I was sweating but still cold, nervous to be so close to this beautiful, strange girl.

"Look," she said. "It's not your fault, whatever it is. Everyone's dad's an alcoholic. Everyone's uncle touched them where they shouldn't. Everyone's mom left and everyone's sister's a whore or a lunatic. Everyone's sorry they didn't do something, or that they did. Everyone's lonely and sad and cries sometimes." She turned my face to hers and touched her forehead to mine. "It's okay. We're gonna grow up and it's gonna be better. That's what happens in books."

She looked in my eyes and I couldn't tell anything from hers except that she was kind—I couldn't see what colour they were, or how old she was, but I didn't want to cry anymore. I didn't even want to kiss her, though I should have—we were alone and I was thirteen. We sat in that cave for an hour, watching the storm blow down the lake, until I fell asleep. And when I woke up, she was gone.

Bud was up on the veranda, knocking on the door of the hip-roofed house. The same chairs flanked the doorway. I looked for the curly-haired girl in the shadows. Of course, she wasn't there. Then the door opened and light spilled out, framing a tiny imp. She grabbed Bud by the hand and pulled him inside. I walked up the stairs with Thomas and gratefully came out of the cold.

CHORUS

Todd MacDonald, over beer at the Cambie

Why Glory? Because she had tits and tattoos. When she got suspended from school, she didn't give a shit; she had black-rimmed eyes that scared boys, and power over kids that would shame the Pied Piper. I wanted to know how she did it. I watched her all through Grade 9, Grade 10—her boredom, her disdain for our teachers—I learned all I could, watching her, but I needed to get closer to know more.

I made a plan. I had to be clever to get her—and I was, even if my plan was sort of dumb. I just had to be different: I told her I knew where the ancient burial caves were and I would show her, but only if she kept her mouth shut.

"You shut your own mouth," she said, but I had her. I saw her eyes spark.

I took her up the hill behind town, even though I was lying—it was the Kwakwaka'wakw or some other Coastal Nation who put their dead in burial caves, I think—but she hiked up in her army pants and tight black T-shirt, and when she stopped to smoke, I gave her my flannel shirt to keep her warm.

"What's your name again?" she asked me, but she was just acting tough. I could do that, too.

"You tell me." I walked away. She had to scramble to keep up.

I wanted it like that with her—she used the same tricks on the clambering, slobbering boys at school. It thrilled me that she was as much a sucker for it as they were.

There were no caves—just a long, convoluted walk that lasted all afternoon into evening. We took a break for a bottle of wine I'd brought (stolen from my parents' cellar), and a joint I'd paid too much for outside the Friendship Centre. We covered so much ground in that seduction that there was no going back. I couldn't believe it worked, but at the same time I felt entitled—I'd planned it and I deserved her. I made her think it was her idea, and that was the best part.

We made it back to town in time for a party at the gravel pit. I walked out of the bush, out of honour-roll obscurity, into legend: Glory Stuart and me. I saw everyone watching us in the glow of the bonfire—her with her hair a black tongue down her back, me with a hand on her ass. No one could touch me from then on. It made me giant.

At university I wore the strut I learned from her. I found others like me—small-town boys made men by their stories from back home; men with scholarships guaranteed by good grades despite nonchalance in the lecture hall, a way with words, self-certainty paired with faux humility that worked on profs. It was easier than I thought.

I came home for summers, worked at the golf course, and then in the bush, both in minor management positions that kept me out of town just enough to build my allure. It was magic, and it was easy, and the best part was Glory: there when I beckoned, waiting for me.

Ten, fifteen years, though, that's a long time. She's always there when I call, but we both know by now that what we started wasn't her idea. And things are changing for me in the city—taking off. I have a new apartment, a girlfriend. I've been thinking about what it'd be like to be married.

RENEE

Glory wouldn't go into the pub. I sat with Todd on the tailgate of the truck and watched Crystal herd her back toward us, bit by bit. The scraps of Glory's voice were too faint to understand.

"Wanna smoke?" he said.

"No. I don't smoke," I lied.

He chuckled. It made me cringe—chuckling. It made me want to pull my turtle head into my turtle shell and hide. He took a drag on a cigarette.

"I don't, either." He pronounced it "eye-thur." Most people up here said "ee-thur." "They're Glory's. I only smoke them to bug her."

"Why do you want to bug her?"

He paused and actually seemed to consider an answer. "Negative attention is attention, too." He inhaled. "I want to keep her guessing."

"Guessing how many smokes she has left? She can always buy more. Or guessing who took them? She probably knows you did it."

He made an impatient noise and swatted at the smoke he'd exhaled.

I was almost warm enough in Glory's sweater. I half listened to him, keeping one eye on Crystal and Glory and one eye on the car. It looked like ours. It couldn't be, but it looked like it. If I walked up close and looked for the walking-fish bumper sticker, I'd know it was ours.

To distract myself, I said to Todd, "If it's to get her attention, I don't think it's working."

Who would have the baby if Danny was at the pub? Probably the Swannells. I imagined him asking them, the look that would pass between them about where I was, who we were, what kind of parents leave their baby with neighbours to go drinking. I felt like a pane of glass, an empty cup. I catalogued the dings and scrapes in the brown paint on the Honda Civic and chewed my nail down to the quick. I knew it was ours. Danny was inside. I needed to see him. I needed him to see me.

Glory appeared, Crystal trailing her.

"Look," she said. "We gotta figure out a way to get on the lake. None of us has a boat. I bet someone in there knows where Smokey's boat is." She patted herself down for a cigarette, saw the one hanging from Todd's mouth, and snatched it out to smoke herself. His eyebrows shot up, but he tried to stay cool. I swallowed my laugh. Crystal put her hand on Glory's back, but Glory shook it off.

Crystal threw up her hands in frustration. "Jesus, Glory. There's no boat. We're not going out in a storm. How would that help?"

"We'll get Smokey's boat and we'll do sweeps of the lake, north to south." Glory sounded sure, but she looked small in the glare of the pub's neon sign.

"That's just stupid," Crystal said. "You said yourself we can't do anything. They'll do that tomorrow when it's light."

"Tomorrow will be too late." Glory pushed past her, walked up to the wooden doors, and hauled them both open at once.

Crystal stood at the tailgate for a second, then sighed, and we all trooped in after her.

CHORUS
Charles Hardy, Dream Beaver Pub

I know what they say about me. Don't bother me none. They can think what they fuckin' want. It's between you and your maker what matters. I'm deep down with my maker, so I don't worry none.

I come into town and leave town. I left my hometown, my first wife and her whinin', my kids, all the family I known, and I come west. Did them all a service. Didn't know my ass from a teakettle when I was young. I come west and I started again. Still young, just thirty. But somethin' of that shit from before must of stuck because I come out here and I'm still Hardy, still fightin' to be treated decent, like I do to others. I done all I could to start over. Then, fuck it. I just lived. Took what I earned, spent it how I liked. I know what they say about me, but what in fuck do they know?

Always askin' me, where's Glory? Like I'm gonna know. Where's Glory? How in fuck should I know? If I could control her, she woulda stayed with me when I asked her to. Said she never wants to get married. She keeps comin' round all the same, though. Sure we got an understandin', but that don't mean anyone else understands our understandin'. I come in from the bush, she shows up, we have a good time, then I leave. I'm jealous and she respects that—seen me come unglued enough not to push it—and people round here, they know that, too. But what they don't know is I'm a decent man. I'm a decent man with a decent way of bein' who don't like to get pushed around.

That's why I come unglued: disrespect. That puny motherfucker Todd MacDonald don't have no respect for nothin'. What kind of man knocks a woman up and fucks off? I mean, I'm no saint, I left my wife and kids, but that was for their own good. This shit is different. Motherfucker left before his kid was even born, left Glory to raise it, but what could she do? Sing it to sleep? She done what I told her and gave it up. I said, I'll pay for its food and stuff and you just stay out of it. I did them all a favour—paid ol' Mac Stuart to keep the baby, paid Glory to shut up and sing, paid the whole lot of them to grow up and take responsibility, but a man's got a fuckin' limit. Don't come waltzin' back into town, sleepin' with my girl, when you're a brazen fuckin' asshole who don't take responsibility, or you're gonna get it.

CRYSTAL

Inside, it took me a minute to pinpoint Glory in the smoky room. She was already face-to-face with Sandy the bartender. I tugged on Todd's arm, tried to show him that Hardy was sitting farther down the bar. If Hardy didn't turn his head, maybe they wouldn't actually lock eyes, and if they didn't lock eyes, maybe they wouldn't kill each other.

I could feel Renee's hand on my back. She squinted through the smoke, scanning the already-drunk crowd, picking through the people for her husband, I guessed. She'd said their car was in the lot. Todd shook me off, suddenly, and flung his arm away. His elbow flew back and cracked Renee in the chin.

"Ouch, Todd! Jesus." She covered her face.

I watched a man cross the bar in a stride and a half, glasses and sandy hair. He shoved Todd.

"Say sorry to my wife."

Todd turned to him with his trademark sneer. "Pardon me?"

"You heard me. Apologize."

I had my hands on Renee's, trying to pull them off her face. The man pushed me aside and took her face in both hands, inspecting it for damage.

"Are you alright?"

The way he held her face, so cautious and tender, I had to look away. Thankfully, Bud walked up and grabbed me. The noise and smoke and music and people disappeared

167

and I breathed him in, my face in his chest. I didn't even care what people would say or think, I only wanted his arms around me forever. If this night would never end. "You're here," I said into his chest. "How did you get here?"

"Danny Chance brought me." He spoke right in my ear. His moustache tickled my cheek. "You found Glory. How is she?"

"A mess."

I took a step back and looked around. Todd had sidled over to the jukebox. Renee and Danny stood staring at each other. Then, I saw Hardy on his stool down the bar, staring at Todd and the jukebox. That was no good. I peered around, craning to see through the bodies, hoping to catch Glory's eye, to keep her out of the range of the explosion I knew would follow, but Glory was gone.

"Oh shit, Bud." I took his hand and pulled him toward the door.

RENEE

In front of the pub, Crystal directed Danny and me to search the parking lot, then to come around the east side of the building and meet them at the beach. She and Bud would take the west side. She gestured at some machinery abandoned below the pub, and the beach. They took off.

Danny followed me through the maze of bumpers and tailgates—a mess of cars and trucks, a loader, a cattle truck, trailers, all parked in a hurry for beer. He caught me by the cuff. "Wait."

The streetlights cast a faint, flickering glow—flashing suddenly then going out, wavering behind the branches of the trees.

"We shouldn't stop, Danny. We have to find her."

"This is important. I need to just... I just need to say... I want to say you look good."

I almost laughed. "Really? That's what you have to say that's so important? These aren't even my clothes."

"No, not that. You look like you." His eyes were all over my face, his brow creased in the middle.

He looked so young and unsure and I felt strange and unfamiliar to myself, in this cold parking lot in the middle of nowhere. We were so far from what I'd imagined for us. It made my eyes fill. I swallowed. I wanted to ask him everything and I wanted to say nothing, just have everything resolved, his arms around me in our bed at home. Instead I asked, "Where's Thomas?"

"With the Swannells."

It hit me like a slap. "They don't love him like I do."

Danny gathered me up like a bird who'd hit a window. "No, Ren, no. Not like you do." He held me in his arms while I cried. I moaned: moans that meant I loved him and I loved our son and I would do anything to start over, to do better, to hold us all together like we were meant to be. He lay his cheek on my hair and whispered to me. I couldn't hear him, but I could feel it—that this is who he'd been missing, even when we were together—the broken, real me, with no defences, admitting defeat. I let myself be defeated, be gathered up in his arms.

"Listen," he said. He stroked my back. He pressed a fingertip into my spine: *you*.

CRYSTAL

Bud pulled me along behind him, past machine tires taller than either of us, past the hulk of a burnt-out trailer, past grass growing up through the engine parts of a popped-hood Volvo, long off the road. I drew even with him when we came out of the abandoned machines and into the street light shadow of the pub. The lake roared below us. Bud had a penlight on his key ring. He shone it under the deck.

"Glory?"

"Glory! Where are you?"

"Bring that light over here." Her muddy voice.

I followed Bud under the pub's deck toward the sound.

"Bud Shinnerd, get in here and help me. I found Smokey's boat!"

"What? I can't haul a boat out with my hands, Glory," Bud said.

"Get that loader in here, then."

"What loader?"

"The one in the parking lot."

"I don't know whose loader that is—you can't just take someone's machine. Listen, Glory..." He paused, thinking. "Crystal, wait here." He said to Glory, "I'll get my truck."

"Jesus," I said, but I took his penlight and crawled farther under the deck. I held the tiny spotlight on my cousin. Glory was frantic, pushing at the hull of Smokey's broken boat, and then pulling on its stern.

I sat next to her. "What do you think you're gonna do with that?"

"Something," she grunted, slipping on the dusty ground. "More than what you're doing."

"What do you want me to do? Help you get that wreck out? Then what? We get it in the lake and it sinks."

"It's okay. It won't sink. We'll get it in the water and Bud can get the motor going."

"There is no motor."

Glory looked up at me with glassy eyes. She was filthy—dirt stuck to the sweat on her forehead and cheeks. "What?"

"You heard me. Look." I shone the light on the motor well.

She made a strangled sound. I realized I'd made a mistake, but it was too late. She fell. I dropped the penlight and scrambled to get to her. Bud's pickup headlights found us—me, like the Madonna, Glory in my arms, both of us bawling.

There haven't been that many times in my life where I couldn't solve what Glory needed just by being there and doing what she said. Sure, I was always there to pick her up, dust her off, listen to her beak off about whoever'd done her wrong, but this time, the situation was beyond me.

In the end, a bonfire was the only answer. Bud hauled the boat wreck out from under the deck and down to the beach with his tow chain. Danny lit the thing on fire. Down by the shore, the wind was relentless. Bud squeezed my hand, then pulled me close in a hug. "Your uncle got a quilt like this?" he asked, nodding at the lake.

I smiled into his chest. "Yeah." But my smile failed as thoughts of Anton and Tiny came back. I looked at Glory, round-shouldered next to the flames. "Bud, what can we do for those boys?"

He kissed my head. "Not much. Something, I hope, but I can't think of anything. You think of something, Dan?"

Danny shook his head. He shrugged, wrapped his arms around himself, looked out toward the water. Renee stepped nearer him and he slipped his arm around her. Current ran through me where my body touched Bud's, and I imagined it ran through them, too. It could have been Bud's touch making me a softie, but I was happy.

A loud bang sounded behind us. I looked up and saw a man tumble down the pub's rear stairs and land on his back at the bottom. Framed by the light spilling out of the open door, another man came sauntering after him. A crowd surged behind them. I saw Bud and Danny exchange a look. They started walking up the beach toward the pub.

At the bottom of the stairs, the swaggering man stretched his arms above his head. Hardy. I could tell by the bulk and stoop of him. He grabbed the fallen man by the shirt, pulled him up, and delivered a nose-breaking punch. Hardy's victim dropped back down to the ground. Bud took a running step, but stopped when Hardy looked up, rubbing the knuckles of his punching hand. Hardy leaned down and grabbed Todd again—it had to be Todd— and hauled him up and punched him. I caught up with Danny and Bud and stood at the edge of the circle that had formed around the fight.

Todd laughed through blood and mucous.

"Like that, do you? That why you're laughing?" Hardy grabbed him again.

Todd spat.

Hardy slapped Todd's mouth, then pulled back for another punch. "You thieving, fucking, son of a bitch." His fist crunched down.

Todd lay still for a moment, and then his garbled voice came through: "This would mean more to me if I knew what you were talking about."

Hardy kicked him in the ribs and Todd bent in half.

"You don't go poaching another man's property, boy."

"That's rich." Todd sat up and spat. Blood sprayed across his shirt, black and wet. "Didn't you murder your family back east or something? You probably got shit in your closet no one knows." He tried to get up.

"Shut the fuck up." Hardy kicked him in the gut. A sick thud. Todd turned foetal. "Think you're smarter than us, don't you? Think you know more than me? Glory Stuart's mine."

Surprise showed through the gore on Todd's face. "Glory? This is about her?"

"Fuck you." Hardy slapped his head. "Fucking baby. You're not a man. Stand up." Every word was reinforced with a blow.

Hardy stepped back and Todd started to crawl away. "You're just a sore loser, Hardy!" He coughed, scrambling to get to his feet. "Fucking cuckold."

"Fuck you, city boy." Hardy grabbed him by the back of the shirt, threw him down on the ground, and kicked him in the head. Glory's cigarettes spilled out in the dirt around them.

The light changed suddenly—it was like someone had switched on a spotlight. I turned back the beach. In silhouette, Glory was black against the brighter flames of the bonfire with a gas can in her hand. There was no burning boat anymore, just fire. I looked back at the fight and saw Hardy lean over and spit on Todd, who lay still on the ground, before he started running for the beach.

Bud and Danny knelt near Todd, but I watched Hardy go, until two silhouettes stood together in front of the fire. They didn't look real—they were flat in the glare of the fire, small, like drawings in a children's book.

I heard Renee say, "Danny, I think we should go to Glory."

He looked up at her but stayed crouched. "This man needs our help."

"He's going to hurt her."

"Who?" But Danny had turned back to Todd, shucking off his jacket to staunch the flow of blood from Todd's head.

"Glory," I said. I looked back to the beach, where one of the figures had dropped to the ground. I started running. I could hear Renee right behind me.

I felt the heat of the fire on my face as I reached Glory. I reached for her, but Hardy rose up, and fell on both of us like a tree. My ribs crushed under his weight, Glory underneath me, elbows and knees. He rained punches down on both of us. I fought to get away, to haul Glory away, but Hardy was like an octopus, his fists everywhere. He smacked my ear, knocking me sideways with the blow, and suddenly the noise was gone—no crackling flames or wind or waves, no sound, just sheer, mad panic to get away. Stars and static threatened me. I felt on the verge of passing out—I couldn't get a good lungful of air, but I could see Glory struggling, still underneath Hardy, and I had to get her away. I scrambled toward them on the sand—and then Renee threw herself onto Hardy and knocked him off Glory. Glory reached for me and I grabbed her and rolled us away.

When I looked up, the whole beach was streaming toward us—people screaming and running. I saw Bud. Bud! I struggled to my feet and ran for him. I looked back for Glory, but she wasn't where we'd landed. I stopped running, and saw her just as she hauled herself into the cab of Bud's truck. The roar of the truck broke through the ringing in my ears. Over the engine noise, I heard myself scream her name. Glory ground the truck into gear and floored it. Then Hardy had me by one arm, shaking me, yelling in my face. Bud ran up and grabbed my other arm. Both men pulled, but Bud held my waist and pulled harder. We broke away and Hardy staggered. He caught Renee by the arm. She scratched at his hand to make him let go. Hardy reached into the fire and came out with a driftwood board, flames shooting out of the end, and then he froze, lit up bright in the truck's headlights.

Everything slowed—Renee slipped Hardy's grasp and scrambled away. Hardy dropped the flaming log just as the truck slammed into him. The truck kept going, plowing into the fire, and then into the lake. Flames and water flooded over the hood and the windshield. The engine squealed, then stalled. The noise stopped. The black lake swallowed Glory whole.

DANNY

The crowd milled around on the beach; chests heaving, they stamped through the embers, yelling at one another. I held Renee back. She fought me, but there was no way I'd let her go in there. Waves rolled over the truck cab, knocking everyone back. Crystal was in the water, up to her hips, the waves sucking at her as she clawed at the door.

"Crystal!" Renee yelled, snatching at my hands.

Crystal smashed against the truck with every wave. Her feet slipped, and she slid away from the cab, sucked out in the undertow, but she caught the side mirror on the way down and held on. It gave under her weight, and broke off, and she grabbed for the handle. The cab door fell open. Glory tumbled out into the lake and both of them went under.

Bud dove in after them.

Too much time passed—endless time. I felt the concussion of each wave hitting the shore. The lights across the lake came into and out of view with each massive wave. Renee shook, convulsive shivers. It was dark with the fire gone, the embers strewn across the beach—darker than I'd ever seen it.

Bud burst from the water, Crystal's hands gripped tight in his, and they stumbled toward shore. He dropped to his knees, pulling Crystal with him, pinning her to the beach, where she coughed until she gagged. He held her while she vomited. They lay together on the sand when she was through, people leaning over them, reaching in, talking to them to see if they were okay, but they couldn't answer, couldn't stop looking at one another. The clouds broke and in the thin light from the quarter moon I could see the fine, silvery lines of the truck sliding further underwater. Waves broke over the hood, the windscreen, the roof of the cab.

"Glory," Crystal said. I could hardly hear her over the wind. Her head sagged on Bud's arm. "She won't make it."

"Shhhh, Crystal, don't," he said.

The waves sloshed into the truck's bed, sucking it further into the lake. The crowd pushed up closer to us, trying to see if Renee was alright. Renee turned her face into my chest to avoid their eyes.

"Look!" someone called.

Glory stood, streaming water, in the shallows. A wave knocked her down. She tried to stand again, but couldn't get her legs under her. She crawled until she was out of the water, then stood on wobbly legs. Her hair hid her face. Crystal lunged for her, but Bud held her back. Crystal pushed him off and ran for her cousin. She grabbed her and they both fell in the shallows, the waves rolling them back toward the lake.

They struggled and stood, then Glory shook Crystal's hands off. They stood staring at one another, swaying in the waves, trying to keep their footing. Neither of them spoke, but they looked like they couldn't move apart, like they were tethered together with some invisible rope. Crystal opened her mouth and said something, but I was too far away to hear. She brought up her hands like she wanted to grab Glory, but Glory shoved her, and Crystal fell to her knees. A waved knocked her sideways and she scrambled to stay upright, to get to her feet, to stop Glory from walking away. Her mouth was wide open, she was shouting something, but Glory didn't hesitate. She walked away.

There was something brave about it, even though Glory stumbled on the rocky shore. She looked spent, slope-shouldered, her hair hanging down her back, but she didn't look back. She walked through the crowd and away up the beach, and no one, not even Renee, tried to stop her.

Bud helped Crystal up. The rest of us stood in the ashes of the fire, milling around, watching the truck slip into the lake, burnt wood floating all around. I couldn't make sense of the night—it was like all the stories my dad had told me about the town had come true at once, and it was just as brutal as he'd made it sound. Bud's truck was gone, swallowed whole. Glory's brothers were lost on the lake, shipwrecked maybe. I hugged Renee. We were on the shore, at least. We were whole. I tried to warm her up, to stop her shivering, but I couldn't. We stared at the water.

"Danny? What just happened?"

"I don't even know." I was shaking, too—the aftershock of adrenaline and fear. I turned her face to me and kissed her. I held her tight, so she wouldn't slip away again.

CHORUS

Ruth Harmer, notes toward a news article, never written

Afterward, even people who weren't at the pub that night, even they'd describe how Glory drowned, or else how she walked away free.

Some versions told how weirdly high the water was, the way the trees were in it up to their roots.

There were stories that had Glory firing off guns, shooting at everyone, trying to kill someone before she killed herself.

What we know for sure is Anton's body washed up on a rock at the mouth of the Stuart a month later. Tiny was found in the wreck of the boat up in Whitefish Bay. And Glory? Nobody found Glory, but we heard Glory found herself, got a record deal and a hit single.

Some swear she drowned in the lake that night, but lots of people saw her climb out of the water, disown her cousin. Some say they saw wet footprints lead all the way out of town to the highway.

There are other versions, too. Todd, for one, never tells the same story twice. If you ask him, he says he was set upon by bandits—that the scar on his forehead is from a bludgeon, the dent in his skull from a fall from the sky. But too many people saw him get shit-kicked by Hardy to believe him. His brain broke that night. He never told a true story again, if he ever had before.

Afterward, once the interviews with police petered out, and once the rumours and suspicions died down to whispers, there was calm, and it was almost like everyone started to forget about it. Then Glory got caught and the rumours started zipping around again. All that time she was out at her place on Southside. The police had her in custody in no time at all.

DANNY

I didn't lie. I said what I saw, just like everybody else. I agreed she got in the truck. The officer asked if she drove it at the bonfire. I said yes, she did. He asked if she was upset, I said she was. Her brothers were missing. He said she killed her lover. I said she saved her cousin. I told him she saved my wife. She did. I remember it perfectly. Fire. Truck. Water. Renee in my arms. Glory there, then gone. Bud and Crystal. Footprints.

The officer probed for clarification. I clarified. I described the location of the fire, the logistics of the truck-fire-lake trajectory. I said all the things he asked me to and then he asked me about my wife, and I stopped talking. The interview room at the Fort St. James detachment leaves a lot to be desired. I stared at the stained ceiling tiles and counted my heartbeats. Eventually the interview was over. I drove home. Renee had made split-pea soup.

In twenty years, when Thomas is a man and he comes home to ask advice from his dad about women or love and if he's about to get married, I'll say, do it. Love her. Marry her. Make a life together. It won't be easy. Maybe we'll be cutting kindling to fill the bin by the stove. Maybe it'll be late spring, when the ice is off and the air is fresh, but it's warm enough to be outside without a jacket. Maybe he'll have a moustache or he'll wear an old hat of mine over his sandy hair. Maybe he'll call me Pop. I'll say, love is hard work. Love is something you make each day. I'll look down at the beach to where we have our Christmas bonfire every year. I'll say, love is a thing you make with your heart and hands and it's got to be something you shore up all the time, that you rebuild to keep the weather out, and that's where you live, you and your wife—in a changing, hard-won shelter the two of you build up each time you find a weakness. With your heart and your hands. Because you said you would. Because you want to. Because of her.

I heard Glory lives in a halfway house in Vancouver these days. Renee said that all Glory wanted was to get out of here and you can't deny she did that. I bet she's alright. No matter what they say about her.

Whatever she's doing, I hope she's still singing. But wherever she goes next, I hope it isn't back here.

RENEE

We set off one day in July in the Swannells' canoe, the gear loaded up past the gunwales, the baby tucked in front with me, between my knees. The day was perfectly still, the lake a sheet of glass. The Swannells waved at us from shore.

It took us a while to get sorted and get off the beach—Thomas wouldn't settle unless Danny was holding him, and he couldn't hold him and paddle at the same time. We tried it with me in the back and Danny in the front, but the back of the canoe stuck up like a toe and the front rode low and we couldn't go anywhere. Jim laughed at us and helped us move the gear around so the canoe was even in the water. He called it "trim."

I tried, but I couldn't make us go straight. We almost ran into the point, and Danny said, "Jesus Christ, Renee," and I started to cry. We took a break then, and the Swannells held Thomas. Danny walked me down the beach and said he was sorry. I wanted to forget about the trip, but he sweet-talked me, said he had a surprise for me, and he did—he handed me a new journal. I tucked it into my new dry bag, and we got Thomas settled. I sat in the bow of the canoe with Thomas at my feet.

Danny got the hang of steering pretty quickly. He'd take two strokes forward, do a correction stroke or two, and after a time we didn't zigzag across the bay so badly. I tried to paddle steady and even in the bow. I tried to be strength for Danny's direction, even though I didn't want to be there.

I'd suggested a road trip to California, something with solid ground, a grocery store nearby. I was trying to be stoic. I didn't complain. I counted each stroke, and eventually each stroke became a word: *here*, *now*, *us*, *this*, *you*.

We paddled away from the bay and the cabin up on the point and it felt good to leave, knowing we had somewhere to come back to, knowing we would come back, and that this was home. I told myself that. I said home. I tried to mean it.

Danny was excited to see the west end of the lake. I wondered if I'd packed enough for us to eat. Thomas watched the birds from under the brim of his sunhat and sucked on his bottle, his eyes at half-mast. Soon he was rocked to sleep by our paddle strokes. We travelled all afternoon. My shoulders ached, but I didn't rest. I stopped only to sip from my water bottle or to adjust the blanket covering the baby. Once, I glanced back at Danny and the lake behind him was huge, the shore completely gone. It was terrifying. I imagined us from above, just dark dots on the skin of the water, a family-sized speck in a world of blue. I made myself think about the canoe; it was solid, sturdy, full of our gear, our bodies, ourselves. It was enough, I told myself. I started paddling again.

There are things I say to make it okay, but we all do that, don't we? There are ways we make the world more manageable, so we can carry its weight. At night, in the dark, when we're spooned up tight together, we whisper, this happened, then this happened, then this, until we fall asleep. Then we wake up. Together. And we try again.

The spring seems so long ago that it's like I was a different woman, someone who couldn't see how good she had it. I needed someone to hold up a mirror, to show me my own face. Funny it was Glory. It turned out she was some kind of messenger. I still remember things she said to me and they sound so strange—I'll be slinging laundry into the dryer from the washer and I'll remember her asking, you're not running away, are you? Strange that I was always running right at myself—the grown-up me with the shitty backwoods haircut, who can split kindling and can finally ask for help when she needs it. And I need it. Now I ask Danny, or Rosie Swannell, or I get Juniper to babysit so I can have a minute to figure myself out.

There's a name for what I have. There are a few, in fact. And it's not failure. I might call it ennui, if I'm feeling fancy. Some days it's just sorrow. Some days it's the blues, but all in all it's mourning, and that's okay. If you're the type of girl who decides who she's going to grow up to be and you're wrong, it takes a while to get over it. Dr. Matthew said I could call it post-partem depression if I wanted to, but I'd rather not. I'm just taking it day by day and writing it all down.

Today, with Danny and Thomas, I dip my paddle in the water and lift it out. I put it in, pull, and push it forward through the air until I grab another bite of water. I pull our little family further into the unknown. Together.

BUD

I found the CD after work, scrambling around for change for a pop in that dark pocket in the door of the truck. Dan was supposed to meet me after shift, but the foreman wanted to talk to him, so I waited in the truck with the motor running, slipped the CD in out of curiosity. I love those first few seconds of tape hiss—when you wonder what comes next.

"Can you hear me?" It was Crystal's voice. She tapped the mic. "Is it loud enough? Okay... Hi... Alright. Okay. So... Bud? Is Paul recording? Should I start?"

I couldn't help but smile. I remembered that night. A bit of a clusterfuck trying to set up the recording stuff, but good in the end. She sang alone at the Dream Beaver for the first time. Felt like my chest was gonna burst with pride.

"Right. So, this is Glory's song. I wrote it. I never did that before because she always wrote the songs. And I'm playing guitar. And it's her guitar, and I don't usually do that, either.

"So, I wrote this song and here it is. I'm not going to talk anymore...I'm just going to sing."

She cleared her throat. I remembered her fiddling with the mic. I heard glasses clink and a dishwasher start.

"Jesus, Sandy, would you turn that off?" My voice. Made me laugh to hear it.

Sandy's muffled apology from far away. Then Crystal's guitar, soft, slow, growing stronger, and then her crackly, beautiful voice:

She says, "Hey, big boy, I've got a song you should hear,"
and for just one second, you're the only guy in the bar
and you wonder, just like everybody wonders,
where she goes between the songs,
and you wonder if it's her or her guitar,
but you can't make love to strings and wood
you can't make love to strings and wood
like she does.

Crystal's voice, like barnacles and salt water, like the wind off the lake, full of sadness and fear—she didn't sound like Glory and she didn't sound like herself, but she gained confidence as she went. I could picture her closing her eyes as she spoke the next words:

She turns her head and spits,
she swears like a trucker,
she laughs right at you,
calls you motherfucker
and then she's not so pretty anymore.

She says dance me outside,
she says take me higher,
but she's so high already
she's crying,
and all you want is more
all you want is her but she's gone.

The sounds of the bar disappeared. I heard Crystal inhale. I heard her fingers squeak on the fret board, the shuffle of her shoe on the floor. I could almost hear her heartbeat.

She strummed awhile before she started in on the last part.

The water rises late in the spring,
branches rattle in the cottonwood like bones,
and you still hear her voice,
still you hear her voice when the wind moans.

She's just a story they tell at the bar
and you wonder where she goes between the songs,
but she's just some small-town whore and you've heard
stories
she's just some small-town girl, and she's gone.

On the recording, Crystal paused. I looked out the windshield of the truck at the black spruce poking out of the bog at the back of the parking lot. I took a deep breath and shook my head because I still couldn't believe it—that she's mine. She sleeps next to me at night and wakes next to me in the morning. She holds my hand when we walk to town. She buys us groceries and gets me a beer from the fridge if I ask for it. I run her baths and hold her when she cries. I get to be the one she comes to when she can't take it that Glory's gone, that she doesn't know if Glory will come back. When she gets a postcard from fucking Whitehorse with nothing but a lipstick kiss on it, I'm the one that gets her back on track again.

When she's happy, she comes to me with why don't we and can't you and my answer is always, always yes. She's come so far since the spring—she's not so skinny, and she's writing songs. I seen the drifts of papers piled up on her banjo on the coffee table. I watched the wind tip the treetops back and forth, the leaves starting to let go. I counted my blessings and they were so many.

Back on the CD, Crystal took a breath and held her hand against the guitar's strings to stop their ringing. She started plucking individual notes and went through the melody one last time.

Dead silence in the bar. I pictured the last notes disappearing into the dusty fur of the animals mounted on the pub's walls.

Crystal sniffed, "Thank you. Thanks for listening." I smiled to hear the frog in my sweetheart's throat. I remembered walking up to her after she played that night and telling her she was great, but I don't think she heard me. She had a faraway look in her eyes. So I gave her a hug and a kiss and took her home.

The recording was over. Static filled the cab. It was a shitty CD—Paul's no expert—but the song rang in my head. I didn't know all the words, but the melody echoed long after the CD ended. I stared at the cover: a date in black letters, a blurry face and a flash of teeth, a woman's soft cheek against a mess of dark curly hair. It still made me shiver to think of her. She could've kept Crystal for her own. Hell, she could have kept Juniper, too, and Renee Chance, all of us. She had this whole place in her hands until she let us go. Chose herself. But it's a good thing she did. For me. For Crystal, too, I hope.

I flipped the CD case over in my hand to look at the spine. One word in black pen: *Glory*. Not like anyone would ever forget it.

JUNIPER

Papa says I read too much *Little House on the Prairie* and he might be right (he's usually right), but he doesn't notice that it's *On the Banks of Plum Creek* I love—still Laura and Mary and Ma and Pa and baby Carrie but a house in a creek bank! Then a new house with pine boards! Sometimes when the lake is wild I wake up because I hear the roof creaking and I read those books to make the night go away. I taught myself that. I read the bad right out of the night and I'm not scared anymore. Not of the lake, not of anything.

Papa also says that I'm baking too much and he's getting fat, but I'd rather he was fat than sad. I don't say it out loud. I love him so much. His eyes are all hollow and he hardly moves around anymore. He misses his boys so much. I bring him tea and sit as near to him as I can. I bring him his book and I bring my book and we sit on the swinging deck chair and just be together. He watches the water and I watch anything *but* the water. I don't want to be looking at it the minute something crawls out of it. And that day will come. I feel it in the creep-o-meter in my back (that's the zingy part of your spine) and I wait for it, keep my eyes on my book.

Papa says, "Don't worry, Juniper," and "Is Crystal coming over?" and "Let's have beans on toast for supper." That's all. He doesn't tell stories like he used to, so I have to read or make up my own. I try to do that. It's better than stories you hear from strangers. Even out here I hear stories, out here and at school. The stuff I hear at school makes me want to cover my ears and run. That's when sitting on the deck with Papa is best—when they say at school that my mother was a whore and now she's dead, that my mother's a murderer, that my mother left me for dead and my papa rescued me from a Dumpster. That one's the dumbest. We don't even have Dumpsters in Fort St. James.

Who cares what my mother did? Not me. I'm almost eleven and I can make pizza from scratch. Crystal comes over with Bud and I cook for everybody. Next summer I'm going to get a new bike, Bud says, and he's going to ride with me all the way over to Southside. Crystal looks at him with her side eyes when he says stuff like that, but I heard him whisper to her that it would be good for me to see it, whatever it is. Hopefully it's not a sea monster or a sarcophagus. No, thank you. If he means my mother's place on Southside, I can already see it. It's a place I have in my mind. There are windows looking out at the water, but the lake is smeary, all soft and blurred like Papa's quilts, and there are dirt floors and you can hear the waves every minute because the walls don't hold out the sound. She's there. I can see her through the window. Her hair is like a black flag in the wind and she's down on the beach looking out at the water. Her face is away from me, but she knows when I come to visit. She doesn't talk to me, but then, Papa doesn't say much, either—it doesn't mean they don't love me. She says, look at the weather—that storm's come all the way down from Portage. In my mind she says, make me a cup of tea, would you? and I do, somehow, on the little two-burner thingy, in a kettle that used to be Nana's. I know it because I heard a story about that kettle once. And sometimes stories come true. Not *really*, but sort of, because I can feel Nana's hand inside mine when I pour the water, and I can hear my mother singing, and I can feel the wind off the lake when I bring her tea in a sky-blue mug I made out of my dreams.

ACKNOWLEDGEMENTS

Huge thanks are due for support during the writing of this novel.

Thank you to Invisible Publishing, and Leigh Nash especially, whose expertise, and whose enthusiasm for and dedication to this story inspired me.

Thank you to early readers of Glory—each comment brought me closer to the book I meant to write. Most enormous thanks to Laisha Rosnau, whose suggestions and undying support grew the book, and to Fabienne Calvert Filteau, who lived the story with me, from early imaginings through multiple endings.

Thanks are due to the Prince George Public Library, to Cafe Volatire and Books and Company, to the City of Prince George (for investing in trail maintenance and development), and to my husband for agreeing to move north. Thanks to my parents and siblings and friends who make living in here fantastic.

I'm grateful that Jim Henry built a series of trails at the base of Pope Mountain. I wouldn't have survived the winter/spring of 2002 without them, and they continue to bring joy to all who use them.

Thank you to Travis Sillence for everything—I can't even list it all. I am so lucky to share this journey with you. Thanks also to Elly and Emmett Sillence, who endure all manner of dinner conversation and whose companionship and insight I value more than they know.

Fort St. James is real, but this version is imagined, inhabitants and occurrences included. I took a great deal of liberty with the layout and buildings in this story, so please don't use it as a map. It was important for me to name the town so we are closer to my goal of knowing other places in literature than major metropolitan centres, and so you would have the opportunity fall in love with this little northern town as I have. Fort St. James is a haven - one of the most beautiful, terrifying places on earth; it is my ancestral place, and the place I always return to. I'm grateful to be taken in each time I come home.

INVISIBLE PUBLISHING is a not-for-profit publishing company that produces contemporary works of fiction, creative non-fiction, and poetry. We're small in scale, but we take our work, and our mission, seriously: We publish material that's engaging, literary, current, and uniquely Canadian.

We are committed to publishing diverse voices and experiences. In acknowledging historical and systemic barriers, and the limits of our existing catalogue, we strongly encourage Indigenous and writers of colour to submit their work.

Invisible Publishing has been in operation for over a decade. Since we released our first fiction titles in the spring of 2007, our catalogue has come to include works of graphic fiction and non-fiction, pop culture biographies, experimental poetry, and prose. Invisible Publishing is also home to the Bibliophonic, Snare and Throwback series.

If you'd like to know more please get in touch:
info@invisiblepublishing.com